I CAN
I WILL

I CAN
I WILL

BE A LEADER—ACHIEVE EXCELLENCE

SHYAM TANEJA

PRABHAT
PAPERBACKS

Published by
PRABHAT PAPERBACKS
4/19 Asaf Ali Road,
New Delhi-110 002 (INDIA)
e-mail: prabhatbooks@gmail.com

ISBN 978-93-5266-713-0
I CAN I WILL
by Shyam Taneja

Edition
First, 2018

Price
₹ 150.00 (Rupees One Hundred Fifty only)

Printed at
R-Tech Offset Printers, Delhi

Contents

Introduction

If You can Think, You can Do

If You can, You will

Excellence leads to Leadership

Key to excellence: Taking Responsibility

If You can Think, You can Do

A road was under construction and hundreds of labourers were at work. A traveller was passing by the site. He saw one of the workers looking frustrated and angry, as if he was fighting with the stones. There was rage in his eyes. He was doing the work with hatred in his heart.

"What are you doing?" asked the traveller

"Are you blind? Can't you see I am breaking stones?" the worker replied.

The traveller moved further and asked a different question from another worker, who looked a little calm but sad. The worker had sadness in his eyes but firmness in his hands.

"Why are you breaking these stones?" the traveller asked.

"I have a family to support and that is the reason I am doing this hard work," the worker replied. He had a reason to do the work he was doing.

The traveller moved further and asked another worker who was breaking stones with enthusiasm. He was singing a song and doing the same work as the others. The traveller was a bit surprised and enquired from this worker, "What are you doing and why?" the traveller asked.

"I am breaking stones to build a road. Pretty hard work it is, but I am enjoying and can very well visualise

> "*you are the stone, you are the chisel and you are the sculptor of your life.*"

the benefit this road will provide to people using the road," the third worker replied.

Amazing! Isn't it? The same work but different reasons, different emotions and different commitments. I am sure it leads to different states of mind and different results.

Very similar to this parable, the road to success in our life is always under construction. In fact, we are the ones who are constructing it continuously. How we view the work it involves determines the degree of excellence we will achieve and the quality of the life we live. In short, we become the way we think. Just remember we are the stone, we are the chisel and we are the sculptor of our life. Life is what we make of it.

Let me first share a little about myself. I was born in a village bordering Pakistan and Afghanistan. It is not a part of India now. During the partition of India in 1947, my parents brought me to a small town in the state of Rajasthan. They had no choice but to either get killed or shift from there during the partition. I was then just over a year of age. I can now imagine the pain and agony people must have endured following the idea of dividing the nation on the basis of faith and religion.

We were transported in Indian military trucks and dumped in a stable for horses of Maharaja of Alwar. I survived, but came to know later from my parents and other elder members of my family that, sadly, my sister had died on the way.

The new place was entirely different in terms of culture, language and tradition from the one where my family was earlier settled. We started adapting ourselves to the new realities of life — homelessness, joblessness and no assets to support.

My parents were not educated but they sent me to the local government school where I started learning to read and write. I never formally learnt 'how to think'; no one taught me 'how to think' nor was there a subject on thinking in any school or college that I attended. In retrospect, I believe each person develops their own way and style of thinking as they grow. I developed my own way of thinking and analysing and synthesising my thoughts and relating them to the phenomena I was observing. Is it not surprising that 'thinking' — a skill which is an important basis of all our decisions, activities and human interactions does not form a part of our curricula in schools and colleges and is, therefore, neither taught nor learnt by our school children and college and university students? At a deeper level, this lacuna in our education system is an important cause of under-utilisation of the vast potential that each person is endowed with.

Thinking takes place in the form of a flow of electrical pulses amongst billions of neurons, in our brain and spinal cord, connected as circuits. You may like to call these circuits as maps or connections.

It is amazing to know that more than seven billion people live on the earth, but the circuits of each person are different from those of others and are unique. I guess people are endowed with their circuits that make them

> "*every human being intrinsically desires to have more, become bigger & do better*"

unique. However, intelligent observation, reading, writing, reflection, speaking, interaction with other people and similar intellectual activities perhaps help us to refine our thoughts by adding or modifying the circuits that we are endowed with. I am awed by this fact of life. Thinking in the form of maps, matrices and similar graphical or illustrative figures becomes the foundation for actions that lead to visible or tangible results. So, I say, "If we can think, we can do and achieve."

What each individual wants to achieve may be different but I have found one thing common among most people I have interacted during my seminars, workshops or personal coaching sessions. This common urge is, 'We want to make progress and become successful in life,' whatever it may mean. It is almost axiomatic that every human being intrinsically desires to have more, become bigger, do better and become more and more successful in life. This urge has brought us from caves to the technological advances that the human race has made compared to other animals. The journey is on and will continue. What appeared impossible in times gone by, like space travel or a trip to the moon, is possible today. What looks impossible today will be possible in the time to come.

The word 'success' is relative; it carries different meanings for different people — some relate success to possessions, some others relate it to designations.

But a universal definition can be 'Success is achievement of a goal.'

From the above definition, it can be inferred that if we have goals and if our thoughts and activities are aligned to these goals, we are a successful person. Success is related by many people to a destination, but it is actually more of a journey. We embark upon the journey of success by taking the first step towards setting a goal in mind. The journey goes on until the goal is achieved and then it is replaced by a new or a higher goal.

Since most human beings are driven by the urge to succeed or achieve success, I shall elaborate the term 'success' in the following sequence:

1. Success is measured by or associated with the results achieved.

2. Results come by actions or activities performed. Just remember that an action or an activity is physical and is at the level of the human body.

3. Action follows a thought that takes place in the mind.

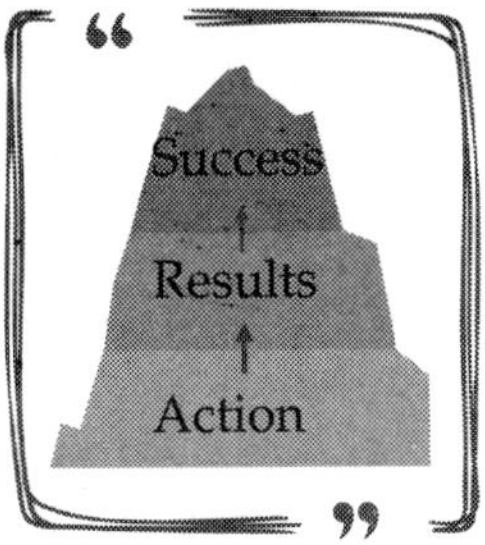

Thinking thus becomes the foundation for any success. It has been rightly said: Our Attitude determines our altitude. An attitude can be defined as a pattern of thinking. It is, therefore, important for one to learn more

> “it's important for anyone to learn more efficient & effective ways of thinking”

efficient and effective ways of thinking. This reminds me of a story I read years ago.

Known for his sensational escape acts, Harry Houdini was a Hungarian-American stunt performer. He was very confident of his talents. He claimed that he could escape from any jail cell in the world in less than an hour, provided he could go into the cell dressed in street clothes.

And every time he was given this challenge, he accepted it and did just as he promised. He was left alone in a locked cell and in a few minutes he would miraculously escape. But one time things didn't go as planned.

A small town in the British Isles built a new jail cell and they were proud of it. "Come give us a try," they said to Houdini and he agreed. He walked into the prison cell, bristling with confidence. After all, he had done this hundreds of times before. Houdini hid inside his belt a special lock pick he had designed. Once the jail cell was closed, Houdini took off his coat and set to work with his lock pick. But he discovered that something was unusual about this particular lock

For half an hour he worked and got nowhere and his confident expression disappeared. An hour passed and still he had not been able to open the door. He tried all the tricks of his trade but nothing worked.

After two hours, a totally exhausted Houdini

literally collapsed against the door and the door swung open. He discovered it had not been locked in the first place! It was locked only to him in his mind. Similar to Houdini, we're the prisoners of our own mind. In order to escape our 'mental jail', we first need to be aware of this and accept it, and then we can find ways to set us free.

So, if we can think right, we can be sure that we have the potential to achieve too. If we can think in terms of 'I can', we can. If we think we have limitations, we simply cannot proceed. But understand one thing clearly — most of the limitations are not created by conditions but by our conditioning. These are the products of our mind.

Sudha Chandran was returning from Trichi to Madras, when she met with an accident. People arrived on the spot and she was shifted to a government hospital. In the hospital, she got the news that her mother had died. The consolation was that she was breathing and was alive.

It took her about two days to comprehend the situation. Sudha had fractured her femur bone. She also had a cut in her ankle which went unnoticed and that picked up gangrene and that small piece of bone ruined her life. She was shifted to Madras Hospital where doctors found that it had to be amputated. After a few days, she went to the doctor and asked an unusual question, "Can I dance now?" The doctor said, "Yes, of course, you can." In 1984 she had a

> "*we're the prisoners of our own* ***MIND***"

stage show and it was a great success. Amazingly, there was an audience of about 1000 people and she went on to dance for about three hours continuously and received a standing ovation. The doctor too went to see the show and asked her who she did that. She smiled and replied he was the one who told her that she can dance. The doctor confessed that at the time when she was asking him that question, he saw her innocent face and was not able to say a 'no'.

This is the power of thinking about two magical words, 'I can'.

If We can, We Will

I begin with a question, "Why will you not achieve what you desire and deserve, if you think that you can?" The answer, to me, appears very simple, "You certainly will, if you think you can".

For example, if we know that we have money or a debit card in our wallet and we wish to buy something, we will not hesitate to shop. Of course, there could be many other factors that can keep us from buying. Human potential is like a debit card.

Therefore, if we realize that we have the potential or power within for whatever we need, we will definitely explore and use it. There is no justifiable reason that we will let our potential remain unexplored and unused for achieving what we desire and deserve, except if we are insane.

The awareness of this simple fact of life does not

require learning any advanced field like rocket science. Then why do so many people refuse to explore their potential or use it fully? Unfortunately, most of the people think, 'I can't'. They doubt their potential and have very little or no awareness of the power they have within their mind. They suffer from imaginary limitations which they have created by themselves that prevent them from trying. It reminds me of a story.

It is about a horse trainer named Monty Roberts, who owned a horse ranch in the USA. Son of a horse trainer, he would go from stable to stable, farm to farm and ranch to ranch, training horses. As a result, the boy's high school career was continually interrupted. When he was a senior, he was asked to write a paper about what he wanted to be and do when he grew up.

That night he wrote a seven-page paper describing his goal about owning a horse ranch some day. He wrote about his dream in great detail and he even drew a diagram of a 200-acre ranch, showing the location of all the buildings, the stables and the track. Then he drew a detailed floor plan for a 400 square metre house that would sit on a 200-acre dream ranch. He put a great deal of his heart into the project and the next day he handed it to his teacher.

> "*most people doubt their potential and have very little or no knowledge of the power they have within*"

Two days later he received his paper back. On the front page, there was a large red F with a note that read, "See me after the class." The boy with the dream went to see the teacher after class and asked, "Why did I receive an F?"

The teacher said, "This is an unrealistic dream for a young boy like you. You have no money. You don't come from a wealthy family and have no resources. Owning a horse ranch requires a lot of money. You have to buy the land. You have to pay for the original breeding stock and later you'll have to pay large stud fees. There's no way you could ever do it." Then the teacher added, "If you will rewrite this paper with a more realistic goal, I will reconsider your grade."

The boy went home and thought about it long and hard. He asked his father what he should do. His father said, "Look son, you have to make up your own mind on this. However, I think it is a very important decision for you." Finally, after sitting with it for a week, the boy submitted the same paper, making no changes at all. He stated, "you can keep your F and I'll keep my dream."

Many years later he told his story to visiting students in his 400 square metre home built in a 200-acre horse ranch. Over the fireplace the students saw the school paper framed. The best part of the story is that two summers ago that same school teacher had brought 30 kids to camp out on his ranch for a week. While leaving, the teacher said, "Look, Monty, I can tell you this now. When I was your teacher, I was something of a dream stealer. During those years I stole a lot of kids' dreams. Fortunately, you had enough guts not to give up on yours."

There are numerous stories like these. I shall only say to you, "Don't let anyone steal your dreams.

Follow your heart and live your vision because you can." The purpose of this book is to awaken you from your slumber and make you realise that whatever you have achieved in your life so far is not the end. You can explore and tap more of your potential. This book will help you think from the perspective of abundance by revealing to you that you have much more power within you than what is required to fulfil your needs. The reason I am so confident about my claim is that I have observed the truth of this assertion with more than ten thousand people with whom I have been fortunate enough to come in contact with. Scarcity and limitations are your own creation. Hopefully, you will shift your perception from scarcity to abundance; from 'I can't' to 'I can'; from impossible to possible; from failure to success. Here, I recall a story of two frogs.

One frog was fat and the other skinny. One day, while searching for food, they inadvertently jumped into a vat of milk. They couldn't get out as the sides were too slippery. There was no choice but to swim around. After a few hours of making efforts, the fat frog said to the skinny frog, "There's no use paddling any longer. We're just going to drown, so we might as well give up."

The skinny frog replied, "Hold on, brother, keep paddling. Somebody will get us out." And they continued paddling.

> "*don't let anyone steal your dreams. Follow your heart and live your vision because "You Can"*"

After a while, the fat frog said, "Brother, there's no use.

I'm becoming very tired now. I'm just going to stop paddling and drown. There's no possible way out of here."

But the skinny frog said, "Keep trying. Keep paddling. Something will happen, keep paddling. Just remember, that god helps them those who help themselves." Another couple of hours passed.

The fat frog then said, "I can't go on any longer. There's no sense in doing it because we're going to drown anyway. What's the use? That is what my destiny is and I accept it." And the fat frog stopped. He gave up. The frog drowned in the milk.

The skinny frog kept on paddling. Sometime later, the skinny frog felt something solid beneath his feet. He realised that he had churned the milk into butter that was supporting him. He hopped out of the vat.

For the last two decades, I have been associated with thousands of people of varying age groups from different walks of life. I have been facilitating them to achieve greater success in life. I am astonished and pained to observe that most of them do not even attempt to explore their vast potential. Very few of the people I have come across live in extremely adverse conditions, so adverse that they cannot even imagine that they have the potential.

However, most of the people have been simply conditioned to believe and say 'I can't'. These people keep wishing or fantasising but are unable to convert their wish into reality. This observation leads me to conclude that 'the greatest waste on this Earth is unused, unexplored human potential.' Over the years, I have developed a deep understanding of the causes of varying success rates among different groups of people. I have seen many people coming from good family backgrounds and with great financial back-up becoming mediocre. There have also been many others who hardly had any resources at their disposal and did not have a great family to support, but they became a source of wealth creation and turned legends.

The question I have been asking myself is why do some people with poor background and meager resources achieve great results and enormous success, while many others born with a silver spoon in their mouths barely manage their lives?

I have identified some enablers that can help people grow beyond their wildest dreams. I have also identified some blocks that can reduce many people to the level where they just survive and confine to mediocrity.

I challenge everyone whose life I touch, including you who is reading this book, with this very short message: "You can." I just want to add a rider to that assurance: "You can, if you will."

Yes! You can, if you will.

> "*the greatest waste on this earth is unused, unexplored human potential*"

I see all possibilities for you to have, become and be what you desire and deserve if you too think so that you can. What you need to be aware

> "in the absence of clarity of destination life is on a directionless path similar to a ship without a rudder"

of is where you are at the moment in the journey of your life and where you want to be in the times to come. Life is a journey and a journey has two points — where you are at the moment and where you wish to reach. In the absence of clarity of destination and your present reality, your life goes on a directionless path similar to a ship without a rudder. Life becomes a matter of chance. In our society, it is then manipulated by the circumstances and other people. We become what others want us or see us to be. We lose an opportunity to be what we can be. It reminds me of a story of a race set up by a bunch of frogs.

A few frogs organised a competition to come out of a well. The goal was to come out of the well first. A big crowd had gathered around the well to see the race and cheer the contestants. The race began. Actually , no one in the crowd believed that the tiny frogs would reach the top of the well. They said, "Oh, the journey is too difficult; they will never make it to the top — not a chance that they will succeed. The well is too deep!"

The tiny frogs began to collapse. One by one, except for those who, in a fresh tempo, were climbing higher and higher. The crowd continued to yell, "It is too difficult! No one will make it!"

One by one all the frogs got tired and gave up except the one who continued the journey. This one wouldn't give up! This one did not listen to the negative yelling of the watchers. The frog finally reached the top. The watching crowd wondered how this one frog managed to come out. They soon realised that the frog was deaf. He could not hear the words that discouraged others to stop making effort.

Sometimes be deaf to others around and, instead, listen to your heart. Believe in yourself, ignore criticism and pessimistic comments of those who could not achieve anything in their lives. You will create a possibility to reach what you set out for yourself. I am sure that if you can think of something and if you believe in it and in yourself, you can achieve too.

When will your wish become a reality? I do not know, for it depends on the level of your commitment to work for what you deserve. However, several (indeed, infinite) possibilities are created the moment you think of something, that's for sure.

In this book, I wish to share my experiences of life in addition to what I have learnt from thousands of people with whom I have worked. This can give you insights and provide you the motivation for becoming an extraordinary person and leading a life of excellence instead of becoming an ordinary and mediocre person.

I am not at all suggesting that everyone can do and achieve everything. But I am sure everyone can be extraordinary in something or the other, depending not only on his dreams and wishes but also on his knowledge, skills, attitude

“*Believe in yourself, ignore criticism & pessimistic comments*”

> *"you have the responsibility to live a meaningful life that will become a light-house for the future generations"*

and perception. You can create possibilities to lead your life the way you desire and deserve. You have the right and resources to live a fulfilling life. You have the responsibility to live a meaningful life that will become a guiding light for the future generations of your family and of society.

Excellence Leads to Leadership

Each time the Olympic Games were held, I used to ask myself a question, "Why does India win only a handful of medals in the Olympic Games?" I still continue to wonder why our country with the second largest population in the world occupies a position almost at the bottom of the medal tally. I am sure this question comes to the minds of most people watching these Games. I have heard this concern about the poor performance of our country in social gatherings at the interval of every four years when the Olympic Games are in progress or are about to begin or conclude. Alas! This standard of performance can be observed not only in sports, but in many other areas as well.

I attribute this dismal performance to the leadership quality and our collective apathy towards excellence. Mediocrity is self-perpetuating as it has a tendency to pull down everyone's efforts for achieving excellence. The time has arrived for changing our individual and collective mind-set and focus on improving performance and achieving excellence in all spheres of activities.

This book is an attempt to help the readers realise their potential for achieving excellence and, in the process, moving towards being extraordinary.

I had experienced the curse of poverty in my childhood as my family was facing continuous difficulties in making both ends meet. I have survived poverty and mediocrity, both. But that was in the past. I now have a degree in engineering from one of the most reputed institutions in India and professional experience of more than four decades in various positions (including senior positions with organisational leadership roles). Having moved from lower to the higher levels in the echelons of the organisations, I can now say with some authenticity that it is possible for anyone to move from mediocrity to excellence, from ordinary to extraordinary.

I am anti-mediocrity because I have lived prime growth years of my life in mediocrity and have experienced the pain and limitations it creates. The mediocrity may be the state handed down to us by circumstances but I am sure mediocrity is mostly embraced by people themselves for their inaction or erroneous actions.

I used to curse our poor state of living at one point of time. Much later now, I have a very different outlook. I must share my observations in support of this. When I was a child, I used to see a local resident run a grocery shop in the town to which we had migrated. We used to buy our grocery items from him. He used to sit on a raised wooden platform. His grandson today continues to occupy the same wooden plank and sell the same goods. The sight of the grocer then and his

> *shift your attention to spot the opportunity that is hiding behind the Crisis*

grandson now has given me an insight. I now realise that the crisis we faced during the partition of the country by migrating to an unknown land, culture and language also threw open to us a plethora of opportunities and the compulsion to survive made us strong. The shopkeeper stayed at the same level and people like us moved out and started our journey of evolution in search of better physical facilities and higher levels of thinking.

I can now say authentically, "Crisis and opportunity are two sides of the same coin." Anytime you have a crisis at hand, just remember that there is an in-built opportunity in it too. You will have to just shift your attention to notice the opportunity that is in the hiding. If one keeps crying about the crisis, one will miss the point. In such situations, we have to interpret and perceive events that unfold differently from our expectations. We have to shift our perception to think from a perspective of possibilities rather than limitations or contentment or complacence.

I have formulated the mission of my life which reads: 'Touch a Life; Make a Difference.' I now work with people to help them improve the quality of their lives. Growth is my buzzword and I strongly believe that growth is the only evidence of life. I work

> *growth is my buzz word & I strongly believe that growth is the only evidence of life*

with people and help them explore their potential. I am confident that each person can reach new heights of achievement if he wishes to and commits himself to it. I am sure it is the birthright of every human being to be excellent in something or the other.

In living our lives, we get conditioned to believe and passively accept the wishes and will of others (family members, friends, neighbours, colleagues and superiors in the workplace, religious leaders, political leaders, etc.). Their will overrides our will and we simply become their unthinking followers.

There is a section of people in society that project the feeling that they have worked hard and contributed significantly to the society during the prime time of their lives. They include people from all walks of life, such as company executives, managers, activists, retired officers, workers, sports-persons, artists, academicians and teachers, lawyers, doctors, scientists, etc. and to a much lesser extent, politicians, too. They nurse the view that they have contributed significantly to the progress of society in many spheres and would relax for the rest of their lives. This view is perhaps fine in the context of highly developed countries. However, I view the very thought of discontinuing an active life without a positive contribution to society as narrow and restrictive. To me, this type of thinking is like that of a frog living in a well — the frog cannot and does not think beyond the well. This is not positive thinking; this is living in a comfort zone to evade exploring the potential we have been endowed with. I am sure this kind of complacent thinking has been of no help to our society and country.

In this context, it is necessary to look at the difference between contentment and complacence. Contentment gives us a soothing sensation. It can also motivate us to do better in the future. However, complacence is dangerous as it takes our attention off our potential and therefore, dissuades us from exploring it. It acts like a brake on our efforts to explore our potential.

Complacent people have a tendency to think along such lines like: 'It is more than enough' or 'enough is enough'. They think that maintaining the status quo is the best course. Unfortunately, status quo or 'as it is' is not a state at all; we cannot find anything in this universe as 'status quo'.

Everything is in the process of continuous change and motion; this is a natural and universal law. We can see only two phases in the life of any organism — one of growth and the other of decline, both of which are marked by change and motion. Complacent people unknowingly place themselves on a declining path, wrongly assuming that they are in a steady state.

I invite you to be a member of the excellence club. Just remember that while attempting excellence, you have to be aware that success and failure are two ends of a continuum. When you choose to attempt success, there is also a possibility of you being unsuccessful. Failure does not come when you attempt and do not achieve your goal; you are a failure when you quit

> ***"failure does not come when you attempt and do not achieve your goal; you are a failure when you quit attempting."***

attempting. Success is to be measured by the risk you take for not succeeding; success is to be measured by the courage you gather to bounce back when you are unsuccessful.

I wish you a great journey of life with background music of 'I Can I, Will'.

Key to Excellence: Taking Responsibility

When India was under British rule, the Indian political leaders and freedom fighters advocated, 'Freedom is our birthright'. In my view, we have been holding on to our right to freedom since Independence.

Had our freedom fighters given the slogan, 'Freedom with responsibility is our birthright', our behaviour would perhaps have been different. What would have been the level of our economic development, if the majority of people shifted their attention from 'right' to 'duty'? I am sure we would have become more competitive and addressed the various challenges of our country more effectively. Today we can see people very conscious of their rights and very casual about their duties.

Watch your words; these become your actions. Repeating motivational words and affirmations to yourself has power. Words spoken with emotion have the power to alter our lives. Try saying to yourself, 'I Can I Will' with emotions and you will notice the change in your performance.

In the second century bc, a young Indian boy at

> *the message to all these dreamers is, have the confidence in, 'I Can-I Will'*

the age of seven was told by an astrologer peering at his hand that he did not have the required lines of education to become a scholar. The young boy went into the house, brought out a knife, drew it where the line should have been and asked the astrologer, "Now, can you see the line?"

The boy was Panini, who grew to become one of the greatest grammarians in the history of Sanskrit — making it so perfect that the Forbes Magazine nominated it as the most compatible language with computer in the world!

Every human being has a special, deep-seated dream. The message to all these dreamers is have the confidence in 'I Can I Will'.

We all have tremendous potential, much, much more than what is required to fulfil our wishes. The conscious realisation of the existence of our potential is the beginning of our journey of 'I Can I Will'. For me, 'I Can I Will' is a philosophy and passion that confirms that there is always a possibility of doing and thinking better than what I do or think at the moment. It unfolds a treasure of possibilities when I start exploring my potential. If there are limitations, they are in the mind. The world is full of opportunities for anyone to tap even in a small measure.

> *The world is full of opportunities too many for any one to tap*

What is required is taking responsibility to motivate the self for continuously beating the best.

Let me recall a personal experience to illustrate how taking responsibility can elevate the status of a person. Some years ago, I was working as a General Manager of a factory manufacturing laminates. I recruited Mohan as a cook for the mess we were running for employees. Mohan was very proactive and eager to learn. He was not educated beyond the school level, but he was curious to learn. I suggested to him to read some books in his spare time; he honestly did so and consciously avoided the company of other workers who would while away their time, gossiping on a range of flimsy topics. Seeing his enthusiasm, I suggested that he learn driving. He went to a driving school and became a good and reliable driver.

On one occasion, a member of the Board of Directors of my company, was to reach Baroda (present Vadodara) from Delhi by 'Rajdhani Express' scheduled to arrive at the railway station in the early morning hours. I asked Mohan to pick up the guest the next morning. It was enough to give Mohan any instruction only once; therefore, I forgot the matter thereafter.

The next day, the Director from Delhi narrated, during lunch after the 'Board' meeting, his experience of the early morning hours. He mentioned that on getting down from 'Rajdhani express', he immediately boarded another train waiting on the next platform. He did not expect anyone to come and pick him up at such an early hour. He, however, concluded his narration with a sense of praise for the courtesy and warmth extended to him and was full of surprise at the way events had turned out.

Subsequently I enquired Mohan about the event. His answer, no doubt, surprised me; more importantly, it confirmed to me that his approach would eventually take him to higher positions.

Mohan said, "I went to the railway station with a placard displaying the name of the guest and stood outside one of the gates. There are three exit gates and I did not know the gate through which the guest would come out. The train arrived and departed, but no one came to me. I then decided to check at the platform, which was deserted after the departure of the train. I thought the guest might be in the waiting room; I checked there, but there was no response to the placard I was holding. I wondered how I missed him."

Any other person, with a background similar to that of Mohan, would have given me a call to inform that the visitor had not arrived. But Mohan was different. He thought proactively and hard. Luckily, someone informed him of a passenger train waiting at the adjacent platform, about to leave towards the station near our factory. He immediately checked into the first class compartment of the train while continuing to hold the placard. To his surprise, the guest was sitting there.

The guest alighted from the train and looked for someone to receive him at the platform, but could find none. He decided to reach the station near our factory by the train about to leave from the adjacent platform. His surprise knew no bounds on seeing Mohan with the placard in his first-class compartment. Not surprisingly, Mohan now owns a company dealing in chemicals.

Excellence is not doing something big it is doing little things better, continuously. It is hidden in doing things consistently and with persistence. Persistence is needed when results are not to our requirement and need change in strategy or methods before attempting again. Persistence needs thinking proactively and spotting opportunities where others are unable to. It reminds me of what I learnt from a boy of 13 years of age many years ago.

I witnessed an innovative selling practice when I was once travelling by train from Jaipur to Ahmedabad. A boy who was selling magazines and books in the train compartment offered to buy back the magazine at half the price at the next station. Many passengers, including me, bought the magazines. I considered the offer of the boy as a good proposition; after all, of what use will the magazine be to the passengers, once it has been read? The boy came back to the train compartment at the next station after three hours and gave half the price to the passengers who returned the magazines and books. He immediately sold the magazines to other passengers in the same compartment. I am sure he did four rounds of selling by the time he arrived at the destination. He had all the books with him and had doubled the money invested on the magazines.

“*persistence needs thinking proactively & spotting opportunities where others are unable to*”

I asked him what he

was doing in life. He said, "I work in the city of Mumbai and am traveling from my home town. I thought of using my travel time in the train by doing some business."

He taught me entrepreneurship. I am sure he must be doing exceedingly well in whatever he is into. The potential exists. The question is, "Are you ready to explore it? You can, if you will."

What will bring out the 'will to do'? This is a million dollar question and needs an answer for us to move forward. I guess our perception of the outcomes of exploring our potential decides our commitment.

Spotting opportunities and exploiting them requires a balance in our perception. Crisis and opportunity are two sides of a coin. What you are looking at decides what you get. You have the power to turn the coin around and spot an opportunity when in the first look you see a crisis.

Here is an example to illustrate the above point. In the early eighties of the last century, I was responsible for installation of a converting plant in the state of Gujarat. The project was time-bound. To add to it, there was uncertainty in power supply and the entire project team was required to work at odd hours. However, a helper about 20-years old used to leave the project site every day at 4 p.m., though his team members were staying for quite some time after the official duty hours. When I asked the helper why he did not stay back at the project beyond 4 p.m., he answered firmly that he got tired and would not work beyond eight hours. I immediately fired him from the project.

Four years later, I accompanied a guest after dinner to a paan (betel leaf) shop. The shop was about 3 kilometres away from the project site and it was about half past eleven in the night.

I asked the shopkeeper, who greeted me profusely, to prepare two paans. When he was making the paans and I got busy talking to the guest, it suddenly flashed to me that the shopkeeper was the one whom I had fired earlier due to his reluctance to work beyond eight hours. The boy confirmed my doubt.

In response to my question on how he could work at midnight, he said, "Sir, this is my own business."

His attention had shifted to income when he started his own small venture instead of the clock when he perceived he was working for someone else. His reply had an important lesson on the relationship between the efforts of a person and his sense of ownership.

Lock to the door of excellence has a very small key: Take Responsibility. Unless you feel responsible that your life is in your hands and you can make it the one you desire and deserve, nothing different will happen. If you keep doing and thinking what you have always been doing uptil now, you will get the same results. For growth and desired success that can lead to you excellence, you have to change your actions and thinking. The power is within you. You Can, if You Will.

❑

I Can

Self-image 'I can'

Why mediocrity is in abundance and excellence scarce?

Role of habits and attitudes

- What is 'Habit'?
- What is 'Attitude'?
- How are Habits and Attitude formed
- Changing Habits and Attitude

Your Powerhouse, your mind

- Conscious and Subconscious Minds
- Affirmation
- Visualisation

Human brain

Knowledge, skill and talent

Human potential

Perception creates reality

Conditioning shapes perception

Self-image 'I Can'

Your self–image is genuine self–respect and a positive mental picture of yourself. Success in any endeavour is a function of this real self-image. We all have our image in our minds. In fact, each person has three images in their minds. Just verify yourself that you hold three images of yourself in your mind.

1. First, who do you think you are.

2. Second, how you would like others to see you as.

3. The third, who you truly are.

Who you think you are makes a tremendous difference in your performance. Depending upon the perception you have and the habits and attitudes you have cultivated over the period, you may hold 'I can' or 'I can't' image about yourself.

'I can' self-image comes from your competency — a combination of knowledge, skill, talent and your attitudes and perception. You have to begin with your realisation of your vast, unexplored potential. Thinking in terms of 'I can' helps you perceive possibilities and not limitations. By thinking 'I can', you will automatically ask yourself, 'How can it be achieved', instead of explaining, 'Why it cannot be'.

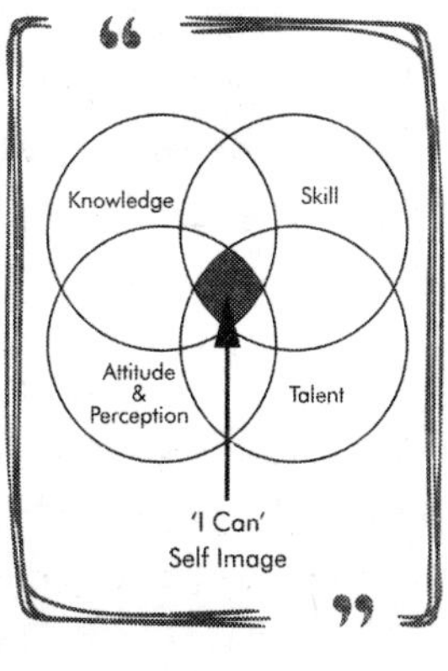

This thought fills you with

> "*If you think of yourself as a failure you will fail no matter how hard you consciously try*"

confidence and sets in motion a positive expectancy by perceiving 'I can' image. Though the size of the challenge you face does not shrink but 'I can' enhances your internal power to face the challenge.

In contrast, a poor self-image or thinking that 'I can't' sets up an invisible barrier and you create your own limitations. At the subconscious level, you will say, "That is all!" and will resort to giving reasons as to "why you can't'! This image produces uncertainty, fear, doubt and worry. Procrastination sets in, making you postpone facing the challenge you have. With a low self-image, you lose respect for yourself. When you don't respect yourself and your potential, others can't respect you either and the road to excellence gets blocked.

Countless people having all the traits that can make them excellent and extraordinary are being pulled back with an 'I can't' self-image and so are destined to lead a life of mediocrity.

Though you cannot rise above your self-image, you can, of course, make efforts to change it. If you think, 'I can't' you are correct. If you believe 'I can', you are absolutely correct.

You think and act like the person you perceive yourself to be. If you think of yourself as a failure, you will fail, no matter how hard you consciously try. You may sometimes accidentally outperform your own self–

image, but you will quickly re-adjust to the self-image you hold for yourself.

If you think you are a failure, you are;
If you think you can't, you won't.
Success is not attempted by every woman or man;
Ultimately it is the one who thinks 'I can'.
If you think you are a success, you are;
If you think you can, you will.
Success is not achieved by a trick or a skill;
Ultimately successful is the one who thinks 'I will'.

Thus, the first thing that needs to be strengthened for achieving excellence is a strong 'I can' self–image. You must, thus, learn to appreciate your potential and the importance of the role it can play in your life. Therefore, you have to consider altering your perception and your attitude about yourself reach new heights of success leading to excellence and assuming a leadership role.

The first step you can take for altering your self-image to a more positive one is compiling a list of achievements you have made so far. I am usually amazed to see people not being able to write their accomplishments in the sessions I conduct. People who have lived for many decades of their lives cannot make a list of even 10 achievements in their lives. Have they lived without any achievements? No, it is not so. In fact, they have not made a note of whatever little they have achieved. In the classroom setting, I usually ask people to write their accomplishments, from the time they got up until that particular hour of the day. Usually they are able to think of many within a span of just a few hours of a day. But when it comes to life, they are

> "*yout must learn to appeciate & respect yourself*"

lost. Actually they have not focussed on achievements; they have focussed on what is not there. I remind them of one basic principle — 'what you focus upon expands'. If you focus on your achievements, they too will expand."

Now, for a few minutes, stop reading this book and start recalling your victories and accomplishments in your life so far. Just jot them down on a paper and you will be overwhelmed by the sheer number. If you make a note of your accomplishments on a daily basis, you will be even more astonished at your daily victories, small and big. Since you have not been keeping a diary of such victories, you are unable to recall. Despite our daily victories in life, most of us have been conditioned to focus on 'what is not there', instead of 'what is there'. Such people ignore the small victories of their lives that happen almost on a daily basis. They miss living life!

Most people have a big doubt in their potential and powers. They have attempted and not succeeded in their previous endevours. Rather than persisting and changing their act, they quit attempting. We are conditioned to think that the alternative to success is failure only. In actual fact, failure comes only when you stop making efforts to persist with your goals.

Rest assured, you are unique in all creation; nowhere on Earth is there another one like you. Thus, you must learn to appreciate and respect yourself. You must appreciate that excellence demands setting stretch goals and in attempting such goals, you are likely not to succeed in the first attempt. Study of great and successful people reveals that they did not walk on a smooth road for their success. They had their ups and downs. The only common factor is their quality of persistence. Persistence is a necessary quality for reaching excellence. Do you know that T.A. Edison conducted and failed at more than a few thousand experiments before he succeeded in inventing the incandescent lamp? He used to say, "Aha, I know one more method that does not work." He always thought 'he can' and he did. Even today, he holds the highest number of registered patents an individual has got in his name.

You are unique and therefore comparing yourself with anyone else is also irrelevant when it comes to exploring and using your potential. Our cultural conditioning makes us ponder about what others think, say, or do. This keeps us from exploring our powers. Just remember that in the unfolding of events and through a process of evolution of yourself, you can make your unique contribution of adding value to yourself and to others in the world.

In a seminar, once I asked a question from the audience while holding a thousand rupee note in my hand, "Who would like to have this without any conditions attached?" This incidence took place before demonetisation of the note on 8th November, 2016.

Initially, people were sceptical as to why I was giving the money. But gradually, some hands went up.

Then I said, "I am going to give this note to one of you but first, let me do this." I crumpled the currency "*there are times you may feel that you are worthless. But just remember, no matter what happens, you will never lose your value unless you think so*"

note with my hands. I asked again, "Who still wants it?" Still the hands went up in the air.

"Well," I again said, "what if I do this?" And I dropped the note on the ground. I picked up the crumpled and dirty note and asked again, "Now who still wants it?" Still the hands went into the air. I summarised, "My friends, you have all learned a very valuable lesson. No matter what I did to the money, you still wanted it because it did not decrease in value. It was still worth one thousand."

Many times in our lives, we are ignored, ridiculed, insulted and floored by others over the decisions we make and actions we take. Those are the times we may feel that we are worthless. But just remember, no matter what happens, you will never lose your value unless you think so. You are special, don't ever forget it!

I ask a question to the people I coach, "Have you taken birth with some objectives or your presence in this universe is accidental?" It is a difficult and unusual question. Think, if you have ever asked this to yourself. In my opinion, everything is planned and happens meticulously as per the plan.

You and I are here to fulfil the obligations we have decided to. If you flow with this idea and are able to recall the purpose, you can fulfil the obligation of your presence in the universe. You, then, can complete the assignment with which you took this birth.

Why Mediocrity is in Abundance and Excellence is Scarce?

I work with people in the workshops, seminars and programes I conduct. I observe mediocrity in their results and thoughts in quite abundance. I wonder and ask myself, "Why do most people stay as mediocre in whatever they do? Is excellence the privilege of a selected few and do they alone have the access to the formula of success?" I conclude that "mediocrity happens by choice made by most people on the basis of their conditioning and conditions."

So, what is the secret to being excellent and achieving great success? The secret of great success is not hidden in education, intelligence, age, gender, luck and access to resources like money or people. It lies in recognising the vast unexplored potential and making a commitment to do whatsoever is required to realise your vision.

Every human being has the potential to be excellent and extraordinary. However, each person is unique and can excel in some or a few areas. It is very rare that someone can excel in many things and everywhere.

From my interaction with thousands of people of different age groups and professions, I find that all of us have our dreams, desires, wishes, hopes and aspirations for future. Humans are endowed with this unique faculty of imagination. During the discussions, some

I believe that people run away from their responsibility for their lives

people are initially reluctant to share their wishes and dreams for their future, but sooner or later, they admit that they do have wishes to fulfil. Many wish to leave some mark of their presence in the world. Many others express desires in the nature of possessions or positions. Very few, strangely enough, had desires for being. It was not at all surprising that the majority of people are not even aware that unless one works for being, having (possessions) and becoming (positions) are difficult to achieve and sustain.

The obvious question, then, is, "Why mediocrity is in abundance and excellence so rare?" Each one has a narrative to justify why(s)he is not in the zone of excellence. But, the most common assumption among most people is that they don't have the potential or capability to rise in life. People tend to justify this assumption by attributing it to god, destiny, karma and other similar beliefs. I believe that people run away from their responsibility for their lives.

Let me discuss in detail all the factors that can help us to travel the journey of excellence. Our awareness about these will help we understand ourself better and it can become a foundation of our 'I can'.

Role of Habits and Attitudes

Greek philosopher Aristotle said, "We are what we repeatedly do. Excellence, then, is not an act, but a habit." It is true that our habits will determine whether we excel or remain mediocre.

Habits definitely have the power to make us or break us. Take it, train it, be firm with it and the habit will put the world at our feet. Be casual with it and a habit can destroy us.

Thus, habits of action play an important role in shaping our personality and character and consequently our success and quality of life.

What is 'Habit'?

Habit is like a rope made, often unconsciously, strand by strand on a daily basis. Once formed, our habits make us effective or ineffective, successful or unsuccessful. It is not as easy to break a habit as is to make it. Write the word habit and take away H from it. 'A bit' remains. Take away A and 'Bit' remains; take away 'B' and 'it' remains.

Similarly, in actual practice, it is difficult to break free from a habit. In my estimation, as much as 98 per cent of what we think and do each day is out of our habits. Although most of our habits like eating, talking, walking, and reading are useful to deal with routines of life but some habits may act as obstacles in our journey of excellence.

> *"Approximately as much as 98 % of what we think & do each day is by habits"*

Since habits are a powerful factor for success, or failure, in life, we have to examine consciously what we are thinking and doing unconsciously.

Habits are not only restricted to individuals. Families, societies and organisations also have formed their own habits and are governed by these. One can work on the key habits in these groups of people and change the results substantially. In our society one habit I have commonly observed is talking ill about people in their absence. I wish we could learn from what Socrates did centuries ago.

Socrates was a great philosopher of his time. One day an acquaintance met him and said, "Do you know what I just heard about your friend?" "Hold on a minute," Socrates replied. "Before telling me anything I'd like you to pass my triple filter test."

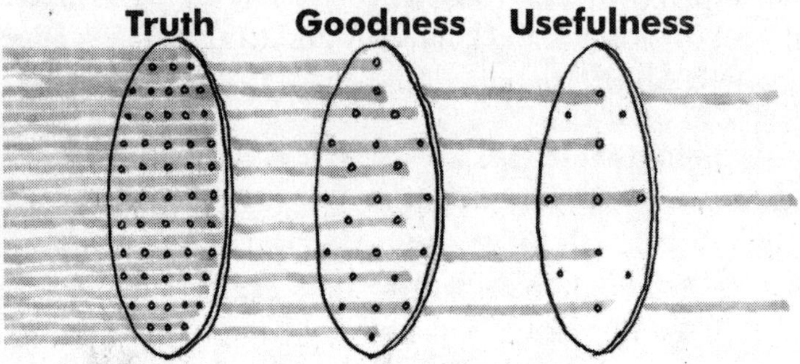

"Triple filter?" "That's right," Socrates continued. "Before you talk to me about my friend, it might be a good idea to take a moment and filter what you're going to say. That's why I call it the triple filter test. The first filter is truth. Have you made absolutely sure that what you are about to tell me is true?"

"No," the man said, "actually I just heard about it and..."

"All right," said Socrates. "So you don't really know if it's true or not. Now let's try the second filter, the filter of goodness. Is what you are going to tell me about my friend something good?"

"No, on the contrary..."

"So," Socrates continued, "you want to tell me something bad about him, but you're not certain it's true. You may still pass the test though, because there's one filter left. The third filter is the filter of usefulness, is what you want to tell me about my friend going to be useful to me?"

"No, not really."

"Well," concluded Socrates, "if what you want to tell me is neither true nor good nor even useful, why tell it to me at all?"

What is 'Attitude'?

> ***"habits include both that of thinking & of action. Action is at the level of the gross body. Attitude is at the mental state or subtle body"***

American psychologist and philosopher William James said: "The greatest discovery of my generation is that man can alter his life simply by altering his attitude." How true! Remember that habits include both thoughts and actions.

While action is at the level of the gross body, attitude is a mental state or subtle body.

How Are Habits and Attitude Formed

We are not born with habits. Since birth, we are forming and breaking habits. When we deal with a new situation, we respond by making a conscious choice. If the consequence of the choice is satisfactory, the response is stored in our mind at the subconscious level. This response is reproduced on facing a similar situation again that saves time and mental energy. On the other hand, for whatever reason, if the consequence of the choice of the first time is not found satisfactory, the response is not stored. Thus, we can conclude that the human brain is designed to standardise its thoughts and actions. This is one reason that most people live an unconscious life driven by habits and attitudes. Attitudes are habits of thinking and formed in the same way as habits of action. We find a thought pattern that gives us satisfaction and we store it for our future use. However, there is a little difference in the formation of these two types of habits. Habit of action is formed on testing and finding a satisfactory alternative; habit of thinking is a little subtle.

Thoughts, based on our perceptions, have the indefinable power to trigger emotional responses without any testing whatsoever. A thought can give you pleasure or pain, depending entirely on the association you choose based on your perception.

> *saying 'I can' gives similar power to a successful person as saying 'I can't' to a failure*

Thus, saying 'I can' gives a similar power to a successful person saying 'I can't' to a failure. Compared to an iceberg, the attitude is the portion submerged in the ocean of thoughts and habit of action is the portion that is visible. The difference in results that come from our physical actions is rooted in the vast hidden power of mental attitudes.

Changing Habits and Attitude

To become 'extraordinary' or 'excellent' from an 'ordinary' or 'mediocre', it is essential for us to acknowledge that change is possible. In fact, change is inevitable and the risk associated with the change is better than being safe. Another factor in the willingness to change is our attitude toward change itself.

It used to be said that one thing that does not change is 'change' itself. But it is not true any more. Change is also changing. The speed of change is changing. For example, I hardly get used to one technology and a gadget in communication (for example, my mobile telephone) and realise that it needs to be changed. The technology is giving speed to change. I find that a substantial amount of my time and energy is spent in learning the advancements of technology.

The attitude of accepting change as an indicator of growth helps us adapt to the change rather than resist it. One who consistently resists change expends much

> *Changing habits & attitudes demands objective introspection observation consistent efforts & persistence.*

more energy in resisting it than the one who accepts change as inevitable and finds joy in the excitement of new possibilities and experiences.

Why do people resist change? Usually 'fear' and 'indecisiveness' are the major reasons for resisting change. Fear of the unknown and uncertainty cause a natural resistance to change. A new experience by a choice of change might lead to a possibility of failure. Whatever the present situation may be, you at least know what it is like and how you can adjust to it. You may welcome changes in the environment if they do not disturb you personally. However, you will think first of changing other people or circumstances if the change is demanded of you.

While in leading our lives we realise on a daily basis that we can change the way we act and think. Humans are gifted with a unique ability — that of thinking and having the thought process. This is why humans also have a unique power to make or change habits. Changing habits and attitudes is a process that demands objective introspection, observation, consistent efforts and persistence.

> *One who consistently resists change expends much more energy in resisting than the one who accepts change as inevitable*

Change begins only with the realisation that some of our habits and attitudes are hurdles to our success and journey of excellence. We must first recognise that we have formed a habit that is giving us some sort of satisfaction either at conscious or subconscious level. When we realise that the same habit is a cause of concern and dissatisfaction, our consciousness expands about the habit or attitude and its consequences. The change process sets in motion the moment the dissatisfaction overweighs the satisfaction.

Changing a habit may be hard, but leaving it where it is and creating a wholly new habit is one another possible way. The pathways created in our mind by old habits if not used, slowly become less connected. This way, we give less energy to the habit we want to change. The old wiring of the brain remains untouched, and the focus then is completely on the creation of new wiring.

Replacement of a habit by another one is sometimes necessary as a vacuum or void is very difficult to sustain. In the absence of an alternative habit, the motor responses may return automatically to the old habit. The secret of success in changing a habit is in emotionally recognising the benefits of the change and the will to persist.

Change in habits needs three things — knowledge (what to change), skill (how to change) and desire (why to change). Momentum is generated for the change of habit as soon as these three components get together.

> *"changing a habit is like sending a rocket in space. More energy is required at the time of take off"*

Remember, changing a habit is like sending a rocket in space — more energy is required at the time of take off than during the entire journey in space.

For sustaining a new habit, we have to follow the same process through which the original habit was formed, i.e. the process of repetition. Our persistence will depend primarily on the extent to which we gain insight about the benefits of such a change.

Attitude change is relatively harder than changing habits of action. Reciting our affirmations is one of the easiest ways to alter attitude. We must affirm repeatedly what we desire to be. Affirmation has been discussed in detail elsewhere.

Your Powerhouse — Your Mind

In each one of us, there is a world within and there is a world outside. The world outside can be termed as 'super- conscious' or 'collective' or 'universal mind'. It is the source of energy in the form of potential or static one. The world within has conscious and subconscious minds. These two powers — conscious and subconscious minds — are contained in one, all pervading super-conscious.

We are endowed with the potential to convert our wishes into reality. If we recognise this potential the world within will take form in the world outside.

Conscious and Subconscious Minds

The conscious mind acts like a guard on the gate to the subconscious mind. It is on duty in waking hours. It differentiates between true and false and comes to a decision based on logic and reasoning that make it slow as compared to the subconscious mind. Like an iceberg, the conscious mind is like the portion above water — small and visible.

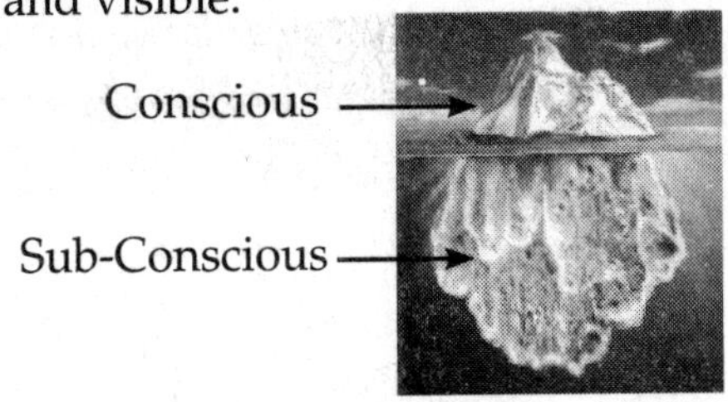

In the context of an iceberg, the subconscious mind is like what lies under the water, huge but invisible. It dwells in the whole body and its value is enormous. It never sleeps and governs all the essentials for living, like heartbeat, temperature regulation, blood circulation, breathing, etc. The Creator has not taken a chance to hand these functions over to the conscious mind, lest people perish every moment because they forget. It perceives by intuition and therefore is quicker.

It accomplishes tasks that no conscious mind has the capacity for. It stores all the data and information of all times, possibly of all lives one has gone through. Thus, it is conditioned and programmed though influence of others as through our own experiences. What we habitually think and do originate from it and bring us the results and consequently determine the degree of success we achieve.

Here, I can mention an incident in the life of a chemist, August Kekule. The French chemist was making effort to find out the structure of the highly unsaturated benzene molecule. He had six carbon atoms with six hydrogen atoms to form the structure. He spent sleepless nights before one day dreaming of a snake coiling very fast and then biting its tail in the last. That was how the puzzle of the structure of benzene was cracked. The benzene molecule had a ring of six carbon atoms with one hydrogen atom attached to each carbon atom. This is the power of the subconscious mind.

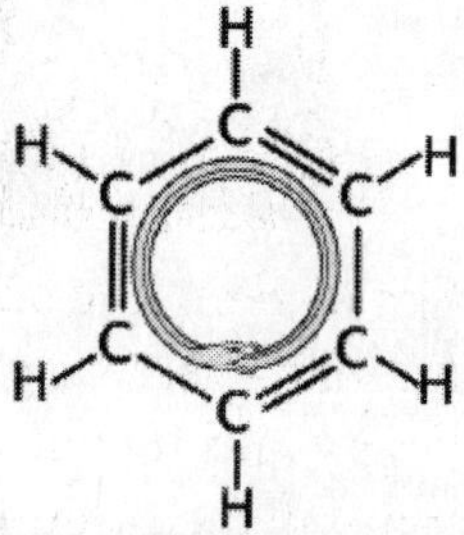

Once a challenge is transferred to the subconscious mind, it starts working on it silently, whether we are awake or sleeping. It continuously stores all the data and information of all times, possibly of all lives one has gone through. Experience yourself by giving a problem you are unable to solve to the subconscious mind. Just before sleeping, think of the problem and ask your subconscious mind to find a solution. If you believe, you will get the solution. Many people do get up at a pre-determined time in the morning by speaking to the pillow at bedtime.

> ***"Once a challenge is transferred to sub conscious mind, it starts working on it silently"***

For being excellent in whatever we choose, it is very important for us to understand that the powerhouse of our mind is within us. In addition, we have to make efforts to explore and use the power for converting our wish into reality.

The good news is that the subconscious is re programable.

Studies reveal that the subconscious is in its peak of receptivity in a state that scientists call alpha state. You attain this state at the time of meditation, relaxation, just before deep sleep and on rising before the conscious becomes fully active.

'Affirmation' and 'visualisation' are the tools that have the power to change our conditioning or programming. Let us discuss these in more detail.

Affirmations

Affirmations can be defined as 'statements in the form of lies that you tell yourself repeatedly with an expectation that these become true'.

Affirmations change our habits and attitudes by displacement. This technique of displacement of thoughts is known and practiced by many different names, like auto suggestion or self-talk.

> "*Effective Affirmations are:*
> ***P – Positively Stated***
> ***I – 'I'***
> ***P – Present Tense***
> ***E – with Enhusiasm***"

An affirmation is a positive declaration of what we want to be. Whether we realise or not, we use affirmations many a times in a day. If we often say 'I can't' we are affirming as much as when we say 'I can'. I keep saying in my workshops, "Please stop saying what you don't want. You are actually affirming it and making what you don't want permanently in your life."

Successful people, knowingly or unknowingly, invariably use positive affirmations to support their attitude and habits. If somehow we have been conditioned to think negatively, repetition of positive thoughts will reprogramme our subconscious mind by displacement of negative thinking. Affirmations work wonders because, by the law of attraction, we tend to live up to what we expect of ourself. This is why the use of affirmation is such a dynamic tool for excellence.

There are all kinds of affirmations — numerical, pictorial, verbal and action-related. The affirmations are more effective when these are positively stated in the form of 'I' in present tense with enthusiasm. It is easy to remember these as PIPE. Make your own affirmations for the changes that will help you become excellent in whatever you choose to be and use them regularly at the time when the subconscious is in its alpha state.

We are conditioned by people around through the statements beginning with 'you' or by our 'name'. For making it more powerful, affirmations can also be framed and recited in front of a mirror, beginning with the prefix 'you' and your 'name'.

Like any other one, we cultivate the habit of making and using affirmations by repetition.

> "*you begin to act like the person you affirm. You literally become a changed personality*"

When we consciously practice the use of affirmations, the law of reinforcement begins to work for us. We begin to look for those strengths and changes that we have affirmed; we begin to act like the person we have decided to become. We literally become a changed personality because we act according to the expectations we have set for ourself. Our affirmation becomes a self-fulfilling prophecy. Affirmations affect our physical well-being as powerfully as they affect our mental attitudes. Affirmations are panacea of achievement and change.

The only requirement on our part is to have belief in our affirmations and ourself.

It is not only our affirmations that work on us, but what others speak about us also influence our attitudes. Some parents unknowingly compare their children with each other or with others with comments that become affirmations for the children. It reminds me of a story of Wilma Rudolph.

Wilma was born in poor family. She was twenty-second child to her parents. At the age of four, she had a disease that crippled her lower limbs. Doctors said she would not be able to walk again.

Her mother, however, said that she was sure that not only Wilma will walk but will win races. Wilma believed her mother more than the doctor.

Wilma created a history by winning the Olympic Gold Medal for hundred metre race for women in 1960. Her story reflects how parents can encourage their children through the power of affirmations to achieve greater success in their lives.

Visualisation

While we affirm for the changes within us, our imagination expands through visualisation to make our wish a reality.

Constant attempts are made to draw our attention towards what others wish us to do or think. Billions of bytes per second are impinging on our mind through the five senses we have. However, we see and hear what we want to, depending upon our needs, wishes and goals. We filter these into our mind, leaving others out.

Visualisation stimulates our desire and operates our mind's filter mechanism. Through visualisation, we draw the picture of our wishes and goals in our mind before they become a physical reality.

Making a vision board is thus very useful for a continuous reminder of what we want to have, become and be. Though we will probably not consciously notice the pictures placed on our vision board after some time, yet our subconscious mind will keep getting reminders of what we have desired.

> ***"visualization stimulates your desire & operates your mind's filter mechanism"***

Human Brain

Let us discuss a little the working of the human brain. Our brain is a connection machine. Our thoughts, memories, skills and attributes are vast sets of connections joined together via complex chemical and neural pathways. If we like, we can call these connections as maps or circuits or wiring. Sets of connections of every person is unique and nearly permanent like fingerprints.

It is estimated that a child's brain contains billions of neurons at birth. These cells grow and die regularly throughout the child's life. These cells are the raw material of the mind that live in the connections, called synapses, between these cells. From the time a child is born, every neuron sends immeasurable signals to make connections with the other neurons. Number of connections run into millions. By the third year of life, each neuron will have between 15 and 50 thousand synaptic connections. The number of connections is too enormous and almost unmanageable. Refinement, therefore, takes place in the next few years. Strong connections become stronger still; the weaker ones fade away.

We can compare these sets of connections with highways and pathways. Used pathways become easy to walk, unused ones become barren. More traffic on highways widens these and low traffic makes these deserted. These connections constitute our mental filters and produce the recurring patterns of behaviours that make us unique.

Our talent is determined by the strength of our connections that define our areas of excellence. Strength of these connections will determine where we will display enthusiasm or indifference. For instance, if we have a highway-like connectivity for empathy, we will feel every emotion of the person we are listening to.

By contrast, if there is a pathway for empathy in us, we will be blind to the emotions expressed, not out of malice but simply because of poor connections to handle emotional signals. Likewise, if we have a highway for confrontation, we will do excellently well in any discussion. If, however, we have a pathway for it, we will become speechless at crucial moments. With adequate training, coaching and encouragement, it is possible to help a person to build a thin path so that (s)he can cope through confrontation.

However, turning a broken pathway into a wide highway is nearly impossible. Simply said, we can't put into an individual's mind what the super-conscious has left out.

Scientists have diverse opinions as to what causes some mental connections to be strong and used more regularly. Some relate this to the child's genetic inheritance while others to upbringing of a child in the initial years. If it was so, how can we explain the existence of different, and sometimes opposite, talents in two children of the same parents? May be, it has something to do

> "*our talent is determined by the strength of your connections that define your areas of excellence*"

with the mental development in previous births!

Knowledge, Skill and Talent

Knowledge, skill and talent are components of our competencies. The distinction among the three is that knowledge can be acquired and skill can be developed rather easily. However, talent is not to be confused with skills and knowledge. There is a limit to how much a person can change. Talents cannot be taught. If we do, we are likely to waste time and effort.

Our knowledge is 'what we are aware of'. 'Things we know' is factual knowledge while the 'understanding we have picked up in living our life' is experiential knowledge. Factual knowledge is acquired through reading and listening. Experiential knowledge is less tangible and very hard to teach. Our awareness of who we are and how we come across to others is experiential knowledge. If we introspect and listen, it will come with time. In the same way, our values, those aspects of life that we hold dear, are experiential knowledge.

Our skill is 'how we do'. Skills are capabilities that we can transfer to another person. For accountants, arithmetic is a skill, for drivers, anticipation and developing peripheral vision are skills, for leaders, 'listening' and 'public speaking' are skills. The best way to master a skill is to practice repeatedly. If we want to teach a skill, break down the total performance into steps and then get it reassembled.

Talents are the highways in our mind, those that carve our recurring patterns of thought, feeling or behaviour.

Talents can be broadly divided into four basic categories: Striving, Thinking, Influencing and Relating. Striving talents explain the why of a person; why a person gets out of bed. Thinking talents explain the how of a person; how things work. Relating talents explain the who of a person; who do you know and relate with. Influencing talents explain the power of persuasion. We will have our own combination of highways and pathways within these four broad categories.

A combination of these four talents, and the recurring behaviours these create, will be almost unchanging, throughout our life. While others will be familiar with our talents, we can expand our consciousness to be fully aware of these.

No matter how much we might desire to be different, the combination will stay steady in us. For developing excellence in whatever we do, we have to make use of this fact by examining our recurring patterns of behaviours. We must, then, make full use of the traits that have strong and broad mental connections. In addition, we will be able to polish these further with much less effort.

> ***“talents are the highways in your mind those that carve your recurring patterns of thought, feeling or behaviour”***

On the other hand, for weak connections, we need to use the complementing strengths of other people around us.

Human Potential

Let me discuss a bit about human potential. Science has not yet developed a method to measure limits of human potential. Someone asked a great scientist as to how much of his potential was he using? He compared himself with a pebble on the shore of an ocean. Hindu scriptures are full of stories that reveal that some people performed feats that are not yet in the realm of our thoughts. Bhishma Pitamah had 'ichha mrityu'. He could decide when to die. Hanuman had the capacity to change his physical size. Abhimanyu learnt about chakravyuh in the womb of his mother. These stories reveal to me that the human potential is limitless. Of course, not everybody can do things akin to these mentioned. It suggests that those who explored, did become great. Written history of humans reveals that we have made it possible to grow from living in caves to the modern man landing on moon.

We can witness the power of the unexplored potential many times when leading our life. I am sure each person can think of the time and instance when they did something extraordinary and considered kind of impossible. We all have such moments in life. It is another matter that most people either do not notice or ignore their exceptional acts. People have performed unthinkable feats, either by choice or under compulsion.

Till 1952, Mount Everest was considered insurmountable and impossible. Sir Edmund Hillary and Tenzing Norgay attempted to reach the top in that year.

They were unsuccessful. Even this feat of attempting the highest peak of the world was considered an act of greatness. Sir Hillary was, in that year, later invited and felicitated for his act of excellence. Sir Hillary spoke three sentences to the audience. He said, facing the picture of the mountain that was in the backdrop of the stage, "You have defeated me this year. I promise that I shall conquer you next year. My confidence comes from my knowledge that you have stopped growing but I am still growing." He was talking of the unlimited potential all of us have within.

Sir Hillary and Tenzing, by their act of exploring their potential became a ChA (Change Agent) and inspired many mountaineers who had a desire to reach the summit. Till the writing of the book, close to 1,400 climbers have reached the peak that include blind Erik Weihenmayer and double amputee Mark Inglis, proving the point that the potential to achieve what appears impossible, is very real. On June 3, 2013, a 15-year old lad from Moradabad scaled the peak, becoming the youngest Indian to do so. Yuichiro Miura became the oldest man to scale the peak at an age of 80. Human potential is limited by the minds of individuals.

'Humans can fly' was considered impossible before the Wright brothers took the risk of their lives to make it possible. On December 13, 1903 Milton Wright, a bishop, was delivering an address in the Church. He said humans were not designed to fly and it was futile to make such attempts. Ironically, on the same day, his two sons, the Wright brothers, were making efforts to fly their first flight. They succeeded on December 17, 1903

> *do you wish to make your own destiny? Very few have the courage to say "yes"*

when they flew their plane, making it possible for humans to cut short the time required to travel distances.

History is full of such examples that make us conclude that limitations are only in the mind and not in our potential. Making a commitment to turn our dream into a reality and untiring efforts are the ingredients to create a possibility out of the impossible.

We will notice that the unexplored portion is much more than the needs of our routines. It is quite likely that the unexplored potential keeps growing with desires and ambitions, giving rise to an assumption that no one has ever reached, or will ever reach, its full potential.

If opportunities are in abundance and potential is unlimited, a question will pop up, "Why excellence is not common? What is it that keeps most people from being excellent and extraordinary in whatever they are into?"

Having understood the vastness of the potential within, ask yourself some questions.

"Do you wish to make your own destiny?"

"Do you wish to make your presence felt in this world?"

"Do you want to have, become or be what you desire and deserve?"

I have asked these questions in the programmes I conduct. Most people hesitate to answer these questions. Very few have the courage to say, "Yes."

However, when it comes to making efforts required, a combination of poor self-image, lack of confidence, lack of competencies makes them believe that it is beyond them to achieve what they desire.

Essential to being excellent and taking a leadership position in whatever we do is the knowledge of self and an understanding of the mighty force of our potential, mostly unexplored.

Unless we accept this reality, unless we can loudly say 'I can', we cannot put it to use. The potential stagnates and remains unexplored. At the same time, once we think and act to explore, it gains momentum like a swollen river in the monsoon that sweeps away every obstacle from its path.

Knowledge of self needs our awareness or consciousness to expand. We need to understand our habit of action and thinking. We also need to be aware as to how conditioning has created our perceptions. Moreover, we must also become aware as to what is not working in our journey of excellence and how to change what is not working.

Thus, management of change becomes imperative for shaping habits, transforming attitudes and shifting perceptions.

> "*Knowledge to self needs your awareness or consciousness to expand*"

Perception Creates Reality

> "response to the situations we face is heavily influenced by our perception"

I must mention a story I heard many years ago. This reflects the concept of perception perfectly to me. Our perception makes us think and act accordingly.

A salesman was sent by a shoe manufacturer to an undeveloped island. He observed the area to be backward. No one was wearing shoes there. The people barely had clothes on them. He thought, with such conditions of living, who will buy shoes here? The salesman sent a message to his office reading:

"No one wears shoes here; hardly any scope of sale; returning tomorrow."

The company after some time sent another salesman to the same island. The second salesman observed the same situation and thought within himself, "If these people can be shown benefits of shoes, the sale will be in thousands." He sent a message to his office reading: "No one wears shoes here; tremendous possibility; send a thousand pairs."

The first salesman saw a problem; the second one saw an opportunity.

Time and again it is seen that our response to the situations we face is heavily influenced by perception. Those who interpret the situation as a crisis and stumbling block, conclude 'I can't'. On the other side, those who interpret it as an opportunity and stepping-stone say, 'I can'.

The perception 'I can't' or 'I can' makes a difference between 'success' and 'failure'; between 'extraordinary' and 'ordinary'.

A donkey fell into a pit. The old owner tried to pull the donkey out in vain. He approached the nearby village people who came and saw the situation. They did not have the necessary tools to lift the donkey out of the pit. They suggested to the owner that better bury the donkey. The owner thought, "Anyway the donkey is too old and would not last much longer." He agreed and asked help from the villagers to cover the donkey with dust and stones lying nearby. The villagers helped with vigour.

For the first few minutes the donkey cried as the stones and dust started falling on it. But after some moments, it became silent. Most people thought the donkey had died. They threw stones with more enthusiasm.

Only when they almost filled the pit did they realise that the donkey was using the stones being thrown on him as stepping stones to come out of the pit. The donkey initially saw a crisis in the stones and dust, but later perceived these things as an opportunity to escape.

> ***"'I Can't' or 'I Can' makes a differences between success & failure between extra-ordinary & ordinary"***

Since perception creates reality, let us discuss perception a little more in detail. Perception is the way we interpret events, situations, circumstances. For instance, if we are wearing coloured glasses, everything we see through the glasses looks coloured. Perception is the way we see and relate to people. Perception is the way we think about ourself.

Walking the path of excellence demands that we are aware of our perceptions and, if required, have the courage to shift these to move towards our goals.

Be aware that your outside world is a reflection of your inside world; you create on the outside what you perceive inside. What you can see and what you will see depends on you, your perception. 'I can' or 'I can't' resides within you, waiting for the choice you make. I repeat, it is within you.

The perceptions we hold are influenced by our attitude and our conditioning and become a foundation for your action, result and degree of success in that order.

To understand perception further, visualise a tumbler half-filled and half-empty. How do you interpret half empty? It may mean:

There is a space!

There is a possibility!

There is potential!

I can!

This perception drives us to look inwards and explore our potential to have more, become bigger and be better. With such a perception, we will act and feel motivated and enthusiastic to respond to any challenge by an attitude of 'I can'. We will see, in fact, each challenge we face as a stepping stone and not a hurdle, By holding an 'I can' perception all the time, you will develop an attitude of 'beat your best, always'. Continuous improvement will ignite the flame of achievement in you.

This perception will inspire us and make us hungry for betterment and excellence hence by paving a path for reaching new heights in whatever we do. We, by this perception, will ride a spiral of success like that of an expanding universe. No challenge, then, will be big enough to dissuade us from being excellent in whatever we do.

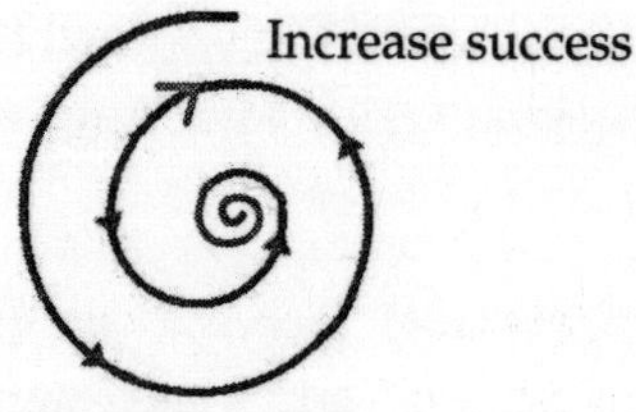

Success Spiral

What can be the other perception by looking at the empty portion? It may also mean:

Dissatisfaction!

Regret!

Unhappiness!

I can't!

> “*most people are conditioned to blame circumstances or other people or luck for their poor performance*”

Imagine how would anyone feel and act with such a perception. It is certainly depressing and de-motivating leading to jealousy with those whose glass appears full or regretful about self. Such a perception may shift focus and attention outside self and blame circumstances or people. Eventually, it may lead them to be casual or develop a concept of destiny. In our society, most people are conditioned to blame circumstances or other people or luck for their poor performance. The perception of dissatisfaction generates negative energy and they are pulled into a whirlpool of failure and mediocrity. These people see every challenge as a stumbling block.

Decreasing success

Whirlpool of Mediocrity

A man who was usually found drunk died and left behind two sons. One of them was a wealthy entrepreneur and the other was a drunkard with very little wealth. Since both the sons were brought up in the same environment, curiosity arose as to how the two children grew to different levels of achievement and wealth.

When the first one was asked, he mentioned, "My father used to drink daily and return home in a drunken state. He used to beat my mother and I used to witness the cruel treatment my mother got. I hated this and every time I saw this happening, I decided that when I grow up, I will not become such a man." When the second son was asked as to what made him in the state he was in, he replied, "My father used to drink daily and return home in a drunken state. He used to beat my mother and I used to witness this every day. What else did you think I would grow up into?"

What you perceive of what you see is what you think and act.

Conditioning Shapes Perception

The universe is full of opportunities, many times more than what usually one can think of. Opportunities are limited by the limits our minds set. The opportunities were always there and will always be there. It is our perception that will make us focus on scarcity. Similarly, we all have far more potential, mostly unexplored, than we think. The fact that humans have survived and grown proves that we have the power to make things happen.

What is the source of our perception? Perception formation is caused by the way we have been conditioned in childhood by others and later by our own experiences. Let us understand the process of conditioning, and its impact on the perception

> "*opportunities are limited by the limits our minds set*"

we have, a little more in detail.

We are conditioned people. Most of our thoughts and actions are conditioned responses. Standardisation of response is not limited to humans only; plants and animals also get influenced by conditioning.

Conditioning of Plants

The Japanese decorate their homes with trees called bonsai by undernourishing and pruning. The plant becomes a dwarf and never reaches the height it would naturally do. Many parents unconsciously do the same with their children. It is amazing to see how good intentions can lead to a devastating result. Of course, the dwarfing is done under the pretext of being responsible and using the society-given power to control the dependent child. Remember, the greatest gift parents can give to their children is that of allowing their children's thoughts to flower.

Conditioning of Animals

Take the case of a circus elephant that stands tied up meekly with a thin chain. The process of conditioning begins when a baby elephant is tied with a heavy chain. The little creature wants to be free and attempts to do so. But, no matter how hard the Little elephant tries, it cannot break the chain. In a few days, its patience gets exhausted and the elephant stops making efforts to be free.

The watchful eye of the trainer makes a note of this change in behaviour. The trainer concludes that

> "*the huge animal continuous to believe the chain as impossible to break*"

the elephant has taken a decision: it is impossible to break the chain. A thin chain, then, replaces the heavy one. With the passage of time, the elephant grows to an immense size and strength, but the huge animal continues to believe that the chain is impossible to break.

Human Conditioning

Humans are conditioned through evolution, for example, to walk on two feet. We are also conditioned genetically, carrying features and diseases of parents. In addition, we are conditioned in our childhood through the influence of significant adults in the family and society. We are conditioned by circumstances, other people and by our own experiences. Can you think of drinking a glass of water from the tap in the washbasin of your toilet? Most people nauseate at the thought itself. Such is the extent to which we have got conditioned that throughout our life we use one method of tying shoes, wearing shirt or trousers, etc. and the list goes on. I am not saying to change the way you do and think; just expand your awareness and note how conditioning is influencing you.

Though most of our conditioning helps us to attend to routines of life without the engagement of the conscious mind, some conditioning acts as a hurdle in traversing our journey of excellence.

Conditioning Process

> "*traits of parents & significant adults are transferred by conditioning more than genetically*"

Parents and significant adults in the family influence us during our childhood. The traits of parents and significant adults are transferred by conditioning more than genetically. If the family influence encourages a child to be creative, positive, persistent and disciplined, the child becomes so and is conditioned to achieve greater success in life. On the other hand, if the influence compares the child with others, discourages taking calculated risks and ridicules creativity, the child gets conditioned to respond negatively to the opportunities of life.

The process of conditioning begins at birth and continues throughout our life. First we are conditioned by others and then our experiences continue to condition us. A newlyborn child is totally dependent on parents or other significant adults around. For the child, the learning process begins by exploring and experiencing. The world at that point of time is full of wonders and a child wants to touch and taste everything that is unknown. Unfortunately, in those moments most of the day-to-day conditioning we receive through family influence is in the form of 'don't' and 'no'. These words are heard many times more than 'yes you can'.

> "*first we are conditioned by others & then our experiences continue to condition us*"

Though the intention of the family members is to safeguard the child from mishaps or do damage to things, the child by such inputs gets negatively conditioned. The curiosity wave is blocked and fear sets in.

Similarly, the society in its endeavour to maintain order, conditions us to follow certain norms and rituals. Most of the times, these rituals are just a carry forward from the past generations without understanding the relevance of these in the context of the present environment. Rituals then dominate reasoning; mechanics overtake understanding. Unfortunately, this happens many a times by sacrificing our genuine dreams and wishes for the sake of others. The challenge is not in being conditioned but the way we develop our perception to deal with curiosity and get straight-jacketed to develop a tunnel vision. This is one reason of creating mediocrity in masses.

Our own experiences and affirmations condition us throughout our life. Three types of conditioning that hinder our journey of excellence are elaborated here:

1. Making Mistakes

In our childhood, we are dependent. We continuously learn new things in our attempt to be independent. Making mistakes becomes part of the learning and achieving process.

> “*the fear of making mistakes immobilizes action and takes a shape of an attitude*”

However, significant adults around us may not allow and encourage us to experiment, lest we make a fatal mistake. Though some mistakes can be expensive and life-threatening, generalisation of not attempting for the fear of making mistakes immobilises action and takes the shape of an attitude. Fear sets in firmly that blocks creative visioning. The desirable attitude, though, in such a situation is to ask yourself: 'How did the mistake happen?', What can I learn from it so that I do not commit such a mistake in the future?"

You will be surprised to know that Henry Ford did not have reverse gear in the first car he produced. The railway compartments when introduced for the first time had doors opening outside.

2. Being Unsuccessful

While attempting new things in life, being unsuccessful in the first attempt is a normal way for development. However, most people label the unsuccessful situation as failure. A parent, or a teacher, or a friend, or a colleague can place so much emphasis on the consequences of not succeeding that our risk-taking ability is confined.

Fear of not succeeding leads to failure. Safety is preferred over risk. Procrastination sets in, self-image is tarnished and self-confidence goes down. To develop an appropriate attitude towards not succeeding, we must perceive such situations as opportunities and stepping-stones rather than crises and stumbling blocks.

When we set goals and make efforts to achieve, we must appreciate the fact that success and failure are the two ends of a continuum. Not being successful is the middle part of that continuum. If we have succeeded

> *If you have succeeded in your first attempt, there is a big possibility that you aim was low*

in our first attempt, there is a big possibility that our aim was low.

For stretch goals, it is very likely to land in unsuccessful zones that can provide us an opportunity to learn lessons. Failure happens when we quit attempting. When we appreciate the difference between unsuccessful and failure, we persist by incorporating the previous learning into our goals. Eventually, we will succeed. Just be aware that almost all successful people face setbacks at one time or the other. Their persistence to succeed makes them successful.

Once we realise that persistence is a necessary ingredient of success, we develop a belief that the response to not being successful is not fear, but curiosity and an attitude of learning lessons.

As a young cartoonist, Walt Disney faced many rejections before he became the founder of the Disney World. Abraham Lincoln did not succeed in his business at an early age of 21. He continued not to succeed till the age of 52 before being elected as the President of the United States of America.

> *response to not being successful is not fear, but curiosity & an attitude of learning lessons*

3. Blaming Others or Circumstances

Have you seen an accident on the road? I have seen many and observed that each one of

> *you deserve on the strength of your effectiveness, competencies, & connectivity in the super-conscious*

the parties involved blames the other. Have you watched the debates on TV channels where especially political party representatives are invited. I have seen them almost all the time blaming each other.

As a society, are we unable to look at ourselves or we have become habitual to blaming others? I have experienced that in our society, the most easily picked up conditioned response is blaming others or circumstances in situations where results are not to expectations. If a student has not scored good marks, most likely the parents are either blaming the system or the teachers or the question paper and seldom holding their child accountable.

Most of the people are unable to link desire with what they deserve. We deserve on the strength of our effectiveness, our competencies, and the strength of our connectivity with the superconscious. When we blame others, we create an environment of de-motivation around us by the negative energy of blaming. Excellence needs taking responsibility for the results as the first step for bringing in the desired results. In cases of poor performance, unless we are able to look at ourself objectively, we will not be able to move towards changing results — a condition for excellence.

The good news is that most of the negative and damaging conditioning of childhood can be reversed. The starting point is the realisation of the extent to which conditioning affects our attitudes and behaviour that affect our success. We must realise that we have the power to change our negative conditioning, as we will.

For this, we are required to appreciate our vast unexplored potential and take responsibility of doing something about it rather than being casual about it or blaming circumstances and people. We are also required to understand that the reprogramming takes place the same way as the programming in the initial stage; i.e. by repetition.

❑

I Will

Creating a vision

Personal mission statement

Keeping commitment

Written plan

Understanding time

How time is spent

Time and timing

Steps to managing time.

Creating a Vision

A man was travelling and stopped at an intersection. There were three roads forward. He did not know where to go and asked an elderly man, "Which road should I take?" The elderly person said, "Well that depends on where you want to go" The man replied, "I don't know." The elderly person said, "Then it does not make a difference, take any road!"

At some point in time, we all do get disconnected from the rut of life and ask questions like:

"Who am I ?"

"What is life?"

"What is the purpose of my life?"

"What do I want to leave behind?"

It is very likely that you have also asked these and similar questions to yourself.

Based on my interaction with thousands of people, I can confidently say that most people have either not asked such questions to themselves or not followed through long enough to get answers to them. It is like a street dog that runs after a vehicle in the street. If the vehicle stops, the dog does not know what to do. Most mediocre people live their lives without a purpose in their mind. They do so because there is no other alternative with them. They don't realize that 'Mediocrity is a Sin' and excellence is their birth right. They don't take responsibility of their life.

Most people live life like a machine. Driven by habit, they live their present moments either in the past or in the future. These people sometimes regret the incidences of the past and, at other times, they indulge in pleasure by recalling the events of the past. Their thoughts continuously swing between the past and the future. They keep worrying about the future or indulge in fantasising it. In short, most people hardly live their life in the moment at hand called present. Moreover, such questions get subjective explanations based on myriad perceptions, for these are not much deliberated upon in families and institutions. Thus these questions, though very important for life, get buried in living the busy schedule of life.

There are some questions that get more objective answers. These are:

"What do I want to have (possession)?"

"What do I want to become (position)?"

"What do I want to be (person)?"

There is a sketchy idea in the minds of most people about what they want to have or become. 'Have' answers relate to what more they want to possess; 'become' answers relate to position they want to acquire. However, clarity of what they should be to have what they want or become what they aspire is almost missing. For getting into the excellence zone or

> ***"ask yourself...***
> ***What do I want to have (possession)?***
> ***What do I want to become (position)?***
> ***What do I want to be (person)?"***

> " *without a vision, you will keep adjusting to your circumstances & get into your comfort zone* "

taking a leadership role, it is useful to ponder over these and crystallise our thinking. If we will achieve whatever we call as success, without having a vision and a plan, we will find very little fulfilment and joy of accomplishment. Success will not build our self-worth and esteem.

Let us discuss a bit more as to why it is so important to crystallise our thinking on such questions. One reason, of course, is that once we realise that we have a vast potential waiting to be explored, our urge to achieve and contribute will rise to new levels.

Life is a continuous process of evolution. Events of life keep unfolding. There will be moments that appear like a challenge in living our life. In such challenging moments, we will win over, adjust or get defeated, depending upon the strength of our vision for our life and the purpose of our living.

Vision, in short, summarises the legacy we desire to leave behind and whatever we want to *have*, *become*, and *be* for doing so. Vision is the foundation on which any future is constructed. Without a vision, the world would not be where it is. Without a vision, we will keep adjusting to our circumstances and get into our comfort zone quickly. In absence of vision and purpose of living, the objective of most people narrows down to meeting the moment to moment needs.

It becomes too late when the realisation sets in that life was an opportunity to evolve to higher levels of consciousness and to leave behind a world a bit better than what was received. It reminds me a story of Alexander the Great.

Though Alexander conquered the world, in his last moments, he expressed his desire to meet his mother who was living at a distance. Doctors said it was not possible. It is believed that he ordered that when his dead body was taken for burial, the coffin should be carried by the most eminent doctors of the time. Secondly, gold coins must be thrown while his dead body was being carried. Thirdly his hands must be visibly open to all visitors. What probably he wanted to communicate was simple: the best doctors can not save you from death, gold coins are of little use and when you leave, your hands are empty

The picture of the future you want to create may not be very clear in your mind. It requires consistent and persistent efforts to bring in this clarity. Nevertheless, it is always useful to visualise and make a determined attempt to make the picture vivid in your mind based on the values you cherish in life.

> *"life is an opportunity to evolve to higher levels of consciousness & to leave behind a world bit better than what was received"*

We have to be clear that it is entirely up to us to make the choice. We can choose to take charge of our life to create our destiny. If we fail to do so, our life will be shaped by our circumstances and other

> *you can choose to take charge of your life to create your destiny. If you fail to do so your life will be shaped by your circumstances & other people.*

people. Remember, there is hardly any relationship of our vision and purpose of living with what other people think, say, or do.

Once we become more clear of our dreams and our vision for our life and once we realise that we have the power or potential within us, we will stop thinking about what others will think, say or do .

Focus on your goals and you will become like an intense laser beam that has the capacity to cut through the maze of uncertainty and doubt. Thus, it is very important for achieving excellence, in any field or area, to have a big vision. Yes, a big vision! small one will not move you as powerfully. All extraordinary performers have had a dream. Dream is not what comes to us in our sleep; dream is what we consciously see and, then, it becomes difficult to sleep.

Erik Weihenemeyr was such a dreamer. He wanted to scale all the top peaks of the world as a child. Unfortunately at the age 13, he became blind. Imagine what would have happened to him then. He, nevertheless, did not lose his courage to fulfil his dream. His dream was so strong that he decided to scale Mt. Everest. He is the first blind person to have scaled the peak. Just think of spending few minutes, even in a known territory, with eyes closed. How difficult life becomes! But commitment to our dream has the power to overcome any obstacles that we may face.

> "
> *dreaming is the launching pad for creating a POSSIBILITY out of impossible*
> "

Ask yourself, "What are your dreams?, What is your big vision for your life?, Are you committed to take actions to convert these dreams into reality?" Look at the list of your wishes and identify the ones for which you are committed and are prepared to do anything. come whatsoever may. Once you sharpen your focus on these, you will be amazed to observe that people and circumstances will begin to help you in your journey of excellence.

Success is achievement of our goals. Ordinarily, the motivation for achievement comes from fear of loss or hope of gain or a combination of the two. The fear of loss is more compelling, powerful, and visible while the hope of gain is a little comforting and weak. Motivation by these is temporary and exists as long as the perception of fear and hope does. In the long run, fear is a de-motivator and hope is lost in distractions.

Excellence comes by 'I can I will' motivation that is generated by our realisation of the vast potential and commitment to achieve our dreams. Our dreams provide us the strength to overcome any obstacle or setback. If we can dream it, we can make it, however impossible the dream may appear.

Dreaming is the launching pad for creating a possibility out of the impossible.

We are all aware that the Earth has a gravitational pull. Any material object ejected from its surface returns to it. Scientists have found that if the object is thrown with a certain speed, called escape velocity, the object will escape the gravitational field of the Earth. Small or mediocre vision does not impart the motivation to the escape velocity. The downward pull of habits and attitudes operates for small aims and the consequence is mediocrity and failure.

Story of Sylvester Stallone is a story of rise from rags to riches. It confirms that if we are committed, we can achieve anything that looks nearly impossible.

Stallone wanted to be an actor. He left his college before graduation and moved to New York to pursue his acting career. He auditioned for almost every casting agent in town with no success. He decided to turn more towards writing and wrote many screenplays while waiting to be an actor. He kept facing one rejection after another. He started writing more screenplays and received similar rejection. Stallone had run out of money and was living in a desperate situation. He could barely even feed his family.

One day Stallone was sitting at home, watching a fight between Weppner and Ali. Weppner was getting absolutely slaughtered but kept holding his ground and coming back for more. This underdog was really fighting for it despite the slim chance he would ever get close to winning. This inspired Stallone to begin writing based on his inspiration from this fighter. He wrote the script of 'Rocky' for over 24 hours straight.

He approached many producers to sell the screenplay. One after the other, he faced rejections. This went on for months. Financially he became so poor that he decided to sell his dog that he loved very much. Stallone waited outside a local liquor store asking people if they would buy his dog. Eventually someone bought the dog for around fifty dollars.

One day a producer liked his story and offered him some money. Stallone put a condition that he wanted to play the part of Rocky in the movie. This was not acceptable to the producer. Eventually he declined even an offer of over close to one hundred thousand dollars. Mind it, it was despite his condition, of poverty.

A couple of weeks later, the producer contacted Stallone again with an even higher offer. Stallone still insisted that he would play 'Rocky'. He however, was firm and once again declined. The offer kept rising just so he would sell them the film without playing the part. The price eventually got to around four hundred thousand dollars. Stallone still declined. Stallone strongly believed that he was an actor and would not compromise.

Eventually the producer offered Stallone only twenty-five thousand dollars and conceded his demand of having Stallone in the lead role. He accepted.

You know what he did first, on getting the money? Yes, he went straight to the liquor store to buy back his dog. He waited three days for the guy to come by and finally there he was with his dog. Stallone offered the new owner of the dog one hundred fifty dollars to buy back the dog but the man declined. The offer kept rising, but again, Stallone knew his outcome and kept pursuing his goal. It ended up costing him fifteen thousand dollars. The dog and the person became part of the movie 'Rocky'.

As you may be aware, the movie 'Rocky' became a great success and won Academy Award for best movie in 1976. At the awards ceremony he read out all the rejection slips from those who said the no one would want to watch such a film. This proves that persistence pays if you believe in yourself.

Personal Mission Statement

More than a century ago, a man was shocked to read the daily newspaper wherein he read his name in the obituary coloumn. The obituary read: 'Merchant of death — the dynamite king dies'.

The man reading the newspaper was Alfred Nobel who invented the dynamite. The obituary was for someone else with the same name. Inadvertently, the newspaper related the dead person with the inventor of dynamite.

This set him thinking. 'Will he be remembered like this?' he asked a question to himself. No way, he did not want to be known as a death merchant. This thought triggered an action and he decided to set aside a substantial fund for Nobel Prizes for peace and in various other fields.

Not that we ought to be concerned about what others think or say about us, we have to live life for ourself. But there has to be a purpose for which we want to avail of the opportunity called life. I believe we take birth with a pre-decided purpose. It is another thing that we forget by the time we start understanding the world. There must be a purpose that human life is designed like this. Irrespective of whether you believe it or not and even if one is born accidentally, the purpose can be formulated to live life the way you want.

A question may come up, "What is the benefit of doing such an exercise?" You must know that 'the law of attraction' works. You attract situations and people to what you think and say about yourself. Then nature will start aligning its forces to help you live your life the way you decide.

A mission statement is a brief, yet powerful, summary of our purpose or reason of existence. It provides direction to our life. It improves our focus and consistency of our actions. We get clarity of our goals from our mission statement. The basic nature of humans is that of happiness. Only when we are not aligned to the purpose of our living that we are unhappy. Thus writing and following the mission of our living provides us a source of happiness.

Nothing is as important in life as knowing the purpose of your journey from 'where you are' to 'where you want to be'. The road to success is always under construction; actually you are constructing it, continuously. There are moments of rest and leisure as parking spots. In absence of a

> "*your attact situations & people to what you think & say about yourself.*"

> "road to success is always under construction; actually you are constructing it, continuously"

clear mission, it is very easy to lose sight of your destination. In such a situation, you have all the chances to be stuck in the little achievements made but the mission helps you come back on the road to success.

When you formulate your personal mission statement, review your wish list. Then write down in a few words in various areas of our life what appeals to you. Various dimensions of life include body, mind, soul, career or business, family and society.

Since writing a mission statement is not taught in institutions and families, it may take some time to learn it. The first step, however, is to bring various words from all areas of our life. Over a period ranging from few months to few years, our mission statement will get refined to a concise statement. Patience and persistence are required for accomplishing this. We must make sure our mission statement is brief and applies to all areas of our life. Also, we must remember that the mission statement is ours and can be altered if the circumstances so demand, depending on our wish.

It has taken me five plus years to formulate my mission of life that read: 'Touch a Life; Make a difference'. Get started today and wait for the time when your mission of life becomes clear and you will find the quality of your life has changed.

Keeping Commitment

> *"people who are in search of excellence are not satisfied by doing less than the best. They do not say 'chalega'"*

A tourist once visited a temple under construction where he saw a sculptor making, an idol of God. Suddenly he noticed a similar idol lying nearby.

The tourist enquired from the sculptor, "Why do you need two statues of the same idol?"

"I only need one," said the sculptor without looking up. "The one you see there is slightly damaged. It happened at the last stage. But I am making another one."

The tourist examined the idol and found no apparent damage. "Where is the damage?" He asked.

"There is a scratch on the nose of the idol," said the sculptor still busy with his work.

"Where are you going to install the idol?" the tourist enquired.

The sculptor replied that the idol was to be installed on a pillar 20 feet high. "If the idol is that far who is going to know that there is a scratch on the nose?" the tourist asked.

The sculptor stopped his work, looked up, smiled and said, "I will know it."

People who are in search of excellence judge their

performance by their superior standards. They are not satisfied by doing less than the best. They do not say chalega. (will do), They have an attitude of keeping commitment to themselves. Commitment of excellence is a drive from inside, not outside.

Years ago when I was a student, I was taking a stroll on the road. Off at a distance I could see a person feeding some powdered food to ants around the place. As I went nearby I saw millions of ants in that small piece of land where the man was sprinkling some food for the ants. I was a bit confused to see the futility of the task, for there were millions of ants there.

I asked the person, "You must be crazy. There are millions of ants and the food you hold in your hand is very little. You can't possibly feed all of them. Why to do for some?"

The person looked at me and throwing some more powdered food over the ants, said,"It sure made a difference to some of them. If I can't feed all, it does not mean I should not feed few."

I learnt a lesson that day. Shying away from the commitment we make for the reason that we will not be able to do in total doesn't mean that we don't do in part.

Very important pre-requisites of living a life of excellence are making and keeping commitment that needs generations of constant flow of self–motivation. We waste time if we wait for situations and other people to be favourable or our mood or our luck to pass by us. We must commit that we will explore and use more of our potential to move towards our vision. True leaders make commitments that they can keep and keep commitments that they make. Making a commitment is the beginning of success. Keeping a commitment is the beginning of developing excellence.

We can feel the difference between a decision and a commitment when someone sets an alarm for rising earlier than they usually do. If there is a fear of loss, people do get up. Otherwise, there is a fight between the mattress and the mind in the morning. Guess, who usually wins? Most of the times, it is the mattress that has the last laugh. Decision is in setting the alarm; commitment is in getting up.

I usually ask a question to the people I meet in relation to the sales of the programmes, workshops and seminars we conduct.

"What is your biggest asset?"

Unbelievable but true! Hardly anyone said that their biggest asset was them. I wonder why people do not consider themselves as asset.

My next question usually is, "When was it that you got your biggest asset serviced?"

> ***"making a commitment is the beginning of SUCCESS. Keeping a commitment is the beginning of LEADERSHIP."***

Most people, again, have no clue. We hardly, as a society, pay attention to servicing of our minds. I have observed people spending lavishly on travel,

> *"body needs exercise & diet plan. Minds needs up-gradation through continuous education & learning. The soul needs improved connectivity with the super-"*

dining and entertainment. But when it comes to buying books that can help them improve or attending class room sessions, they have a very different and conservative attitude. Either they think they don't need any improvement or they are not aware that they can do better.

The greatest gift we can give to ourself is keeping our three dimensions of life sharpened. Body needs exercise and diet plan; mind needs upgradation through continuous education and learning; the soul needs improved connectivity with the super-conscious. These all need effort and taking us out of our comfort zones. Developing excellence demands our commitment on these dimensions of life.

Written Plan

Thought is subtle energy transferred from the super conscious to the individual mind. By transferring a thought into our mind, the super conscious has played its role. It then awaits the matching response from us. It is, therefore, our responsibility to hold on to the thought through some system and make a commitment to act on it at an appropriate time. For this, it is very useful to have a pen and a paper or a dictaphone with us near all strategic locations.

For converting a thought into a physical reality, it is useful to make written plans that include our present situation, target dates to reach visualised destination and mechanism to track progress. By this, we will develop the power to convert thoughts into actions that will take us from a wish to reality.

Why should you write your wish list, plans, goals, and achievements? The answer is very simple. Taking time and making efforts to write is an act of commitment, a pre-requisite for excellence. Universal law of attraction says: "You tend to draw to yourself that which you set out for yourself." You attract to yourself what your thoughts attract. You become precisely what you imagine yourself to be.

In writing our wish list or plan or goal, we become more clear and get involved; our subconscious mind becomes alert to events and opportunities relating to these. Written plans improve our focus by triggering the filter mechanism of our mind to act as barriers to outside distractions and interruptions. By writing a goal, we imagine and create the end-result in our mind that will provide motivation for achievement.

Writing creates reference for future, conserves energy in re-doing and makes tracking of our goals easy. Moreover, it helps us renew our commitment each time we review our plans and goals. In writing our achievements, we get motivated and realise our potential to achieve that helps us stretch our goals and encourages us to add to our wish list.

> ***"you attract to yourself what your thoughts attract. You become precisely what you imagine yourself to be"***

Plan for Excellence

Three fish lived in a pond. One was named 'Plan', another was 'Think' and the third was called 'Wait'. One day they heard a fisherman say he would be going to cast his net in their pond the next day.

'Plan,' said, "I am swimming down the river tonight."

'Think' said, "I am sure I will think and come up with a plan."

'Wait' lazily said, "There is lot of time till the next morning. I will do something by then."

Next day when the fisherman cast his nets, 'Plan' was not covered by the net. But 'Think' and 'Wait' were caught by the fisherman.

'Think' thought of a plan and quickly rolled his belly up and pretended to be dead. "Oh, this fish is no good!" said the fisherman and threw him safely back into the water. However, 'Wait' ended up in the fish market.

Moral of the story is that success and procrastination are enemies of each other. If we wait or fail to plan, we are planning to fail.

A plan must be designed to move us from wish to reality. Setting goals without the relevant and connected wish becomes more of an exercise of logic and words. Chances are very high that momentum will fade away in course of time for goals without the connecting wish as a guide.

A plan assists us to travel our journey of 'where we are' to 'where we desire to be'. The process provides a structure and framework to what we actually do in life for any achievement. For smaller aims, the process works in the mind and it works well. However, for complex and big-size goals, the plan has to be written or typed.

One major reason many people are not able to convert their wish into reality is that they do not know 'where they are' or 'their present reality'. Self-analysis, required to know this, makes them uncomfortable. The other reason may be that they are living in their own world full of fantasies or rejections. Yet another reason is that the process of wish conversion and goal setting is not taught by institutions and parents that well. In fact, for most people identification goals that will help them convert their wish into reality is itself an uphill task. Yet another reason is that people switch from one wish to another, not persisting enough.

We do have flashes of thoughts coming at different times in the form of a wish. "I wish I could have, become, or be ..." are very common statements. Wish appears on the screen of our mind similar to the lightening in the sky. It is momentary and directionless. It vanishes without any utility or purpose. Ironically, it leaves behind just darkness.

> "*wish appears on the screen of our mind similar to the lightening in the sky. It is momentary & directionless*"

"*'your plan' will be meaningful only if it truly reflects your value system.*"

A plan sheet does not stop at the wish point. It helps us convert our wish into a reality through steps as follows:

Identifying the impact of the wish not being a current reality or identifying the anticipated benefits when the wish becomes a reality creates an emotional bondage to intensify our desire. If we answer the question: how does it impact me that the wish is not a reality as 'nothing much' or 'it is okay' or 'it does not make much of a difference', chances are that our wish will remain a wish. It is the burning desire that plays the real trick in converting the wish into a reality.

Remember, the critical difference between the champion and those who finish below the top is not so much of a difference in talents, abilities, or techniques, as it is a difference in intensity of desire. The benefits may be tangible or intangible ones, our list of benefits must be meaningful to us. If the reward for reaching a goal is increased self–respect, or more prestige, or a higher self–image, write it down. This is 'your plan' and it will be meaningful only if it truly reflects your value system.

Setting a M.A.S.T.E.R goal is the next step to convert our wish into a reality, that generates a strong force for self–motivation. Not all goals are equal in importance, time frame and nature. The importance is governed by our priorities. Some goals may be more important than others. Goals may be of long-term or short-term. Some goals point towards possession; others involve

> *goals of 'being' are the ones that can take you towards goals of 'becoming' & then to goals of 'having'*

gaining a position, yet some others may make us change traits of our personality or character. Some are clear and vivid; others are indefinable and intangible. Until and unless we are able to bring some kind of order, sequence and priority into the maze of confusion that constitutes our collection of goals, we will find even those close at hand difficult to achieve. The human mind is such an orderly, systematic computer that it will not function under chaotic conditions.

In M.A.S.T.E.R goal M stands for Measurable; A for Attainable; S for Stretch; T for Time bound; E for Enthusiasm; and R for Realistic. You must make goals that are measurable. Goals of intangible nature can be made measurable by creating a scale from 0 to 10. The other way is to make the expected outcome measurable. Since we have vast unexplored potential, the goal must be such that it stretches our abilities. The motivation for achieving a goal that does not stretch our potential is very low. Too many people, usually the beginners, set goals 'to have' but not 'to be' or 'to become'. The reality is that goals of 'have' nature can easily be achieved by first setting goals of 'become' and goals of 'be' nature.

Once the goal setting process becomes part of you, you must recognize the need for and to work towards internal changes.

One thing is certain: you must set goals of becoming (holding a position) before you can reach the more tangible goals of having. Goals of 'being' are the ones that can take you towards goals of 'becoming' and then to goals of 'having'.

Goals may be long-term or short-term ones. There is a possibility that you may lose sight of long-term goals, say a goal to be accomplished in a period of more than three years. It is preferred that you break down such a long-term goal into small ones of a period of less than 12 months or so. Achieving short-term goals builds your self-confidence, enhances enthusiasm. You get motivated for using more of your potential and to broaden your vision.

A word of caution about short-term goals: is that don't confuse them with low-aim goals. In Gujarat, there is a saying that translates as: "You can be forgiven for a missed target but not for a low aim." There is no motivation in a goal that is too easily reached. A short-term goal is one that is short in terms of the time span involved; not in the effort put forth.

<u>You need to write the process</u> as to how the goal will be achieved and wish is converted into reality. The underlying assumption is that you have within you the matching power of converting your wish into reality. The description of relation between the end result and the present situation makes you travel the journey mentally. Everything is created thrice — first in the super conscious mind, then in the individual mind finally with the idea becoming a physical reality.

> "*over a period of time you will realize that the external hurdles are non-existent*"

You need to identify the hurdles, both external and internal, that can block you from achieving your goal. What can possibly stop you to convert your wish into a reality? Don't create your own obstacles but anticipate them. Experience will refine your skill for this. Keep in mind that you are not likely to reach your goals until you know about all the things that can stand in the way of their achievement. You cannot fight shadows; neither can you achieve bigger things in life without stretching yourself. So make your list of hurdles as complete as possible. Real challenge lies in recognising hurdles that should be overcome. The external factors based on experience are useful to be listed so that you can plan better. However, you have to be careful that you do not create a hypothetical list. The internal hurdles are the ones that your attitude, talents and habits will pose in achieving the goal you set for converting your wish into a reality.

Solutions to the hurdles are introspective by nature. You should be aware of them or else you may seek help to get answers. Over a period of time we will realise that the external hurdles are non-existent; we will find we can overcome any hurdles by actions we take — by changing our habits, attitudes, or perception. No longer will then the emphasis rest on outside circumstances becoming external hurdles.

> "*neither can you achieve bigger things in life without stretching yourself*"

All attention will shift to our own unexplored potential — to things we can control. List your answers in the 'solutions' column opposite the appropriate 'hurdle' and the result will be an expanding outline. For dealing with your internal hurdles, i.e. those of our attitudes and habits, we may use affirmations.

Deciding action steps, both one-time actions or recurring ones, depends on the target dates. There is a possibility of the process coming to a halt at this stage if we do not plan for and commit to the actions required. Remember that definite plans motivate us and help us get definite results. Indefinite plans leave the matter to chance and produce no results. It will also be very useful to tentatively decide the deadline for each action that is planned.

Set dealines for each cation step. A deadline sets an urgency syndrome and alerts our body chemistry. Our observations and response get aligned to the actions subconsciously. A target date creates a challenge within us and we respond to the challenge mentally. The deadline also creates a positive stress in us and forces us to move towards our goals with positive mental attitude, commitment and enthusiasm. We develop the power of saying 'no' to other demands on our time and prioritise our time for our goals. One word of caution about the target dates. Remember you are the master and not the dates. You can always make changes in your plans and change your priorities. The guilt feeling comes only when you procrastinate and are aware that

> ***"a deadline sets an urgency syndrome & alerts your body chemistry"***

you are shying away from creating possibilities to meet the deadlines. When, for reasons like miscalculation, unanticipated circumstances or lack of information, the dates need change, you are the master and free to review and make an appropriate change.

Track the progress. In your journey from where you are to where you want to be, it is likely that you may wander. When this happens, it is frustrating and time consuming to come on track again. The best way is to create milestones and check routinely whether you are on track. Tracking progress on the actions you have decided to take for achieving your goals is a surer method for you to be successful. Tracking the progress also provides you feedback on what works and what does not. You can, then, make any changes required to reach your goals. You also know if you have gone off course and thus need to get back on course. Devising a measuring system also forces you to clarify your goals. Measuring progress may reveal that you need to modify your goals or also if you are working on the wrong goals. Remember, if a goal is worthwhile and is also the right one for you, there are appropriate ways to measure progress towards it.

Once the importance of planning is understood clearly, understanding of the key resource of success called 'time' has to be developed to achieve our goals. For this, we have to have thorough and practical details of the concept called 'time' and know how to manage it for achieving our goals.

Understanding Time

For ages, many people have thought about the word 'time'. Many have made attempts to define it. However, only a few have understood time and even fewer have leveraged time for achieving success.

Albert Einstein in his theory of relativity established the space and time continuum and time as the fourth dimension.

Benjamin Franklin a renowned philosopher said, "Remember that time is money. Do you love life?" asks Franklin. "Then do not squander time, for that is the stuff life is made of."

Arnold Bennett defined time as the inexplicable raw material of everything. With it all is possible, without it nothing.

Immanuel Kant said: "Time has no real existence outside the human mind."

What is time? Though 'time' is the most common noun used in the world, most humans hardly know what really is the concept of 'time'. Is it a creation of the human mind, for animals, birds and plants don't know anything about 'time'.

Defining time is a challenge. However, think deep and realise that time is your life. After all, what is life for anyone? Is it not a period between birth and death?

> "*time is a period for you to have, become, and be what you desire*"

> *people aspiring to GROW find it difficult to find time!*

Time is a period for you to have, become and be what you desire. It is an opportunity for you to evolve to higher levels of consciousness and be a fulfilled person. Achievers in any field have always known well that time is a key resource that can help them succeed.

Most people normally confuse between the measurement of time and the concept 'time'. One aspect we are sure is that time is not absolute but relative. Though we all measure time the same way, the clock appears to move slowly for one person and rapidly for another. Every minute is a drag for a night watchman; hours fly during an interesting event. Time appears too long when you wait for someone; too short when you need it. Minutes appear as hours when in anxiety or pursuing self-development activities; hours appear as minutes while sleeping or in recreation. When you watch the clock, movement of time is slow; when you take your eyes off, time moves very fast.

The other aspect of time is its availability. Though we all have one thousand four hundred forty minutes each day, we can easily observe that those who need more time, struggle to find it. Ironically, those who don't feel shortage of time, have plenty of it. People aspiring to grow find it difficult to get time. On the other hand, mediocre people have difficulty in passing their time. This difficulty pushes them to unplanned entertainment and in activities that are a waste of time.

Why is it that one has plenty of 'time' and the other struggles to find it? Simple! One reason is the absence of mission or purpose of living for the former.

We can conclude that understanding the concept and defining 'time' is a challenge. This will bring up a question: How to manage time when we are unable to define it precisely? Think deeply and you may arrive at a conclusion that managing time is a myth. You can't hold the movement of the hands of a clock to suit your requirements. One thing, of course, surely can be done. You can manage yourself with reference to the clock that measures time.

Thus, essence of time management is hidden in our attitude and perception. The secret of getting the required time (or minutes) is not in finding time, but in planning for it.

The key to time management is in engaging in prioritised activities that move us towards our goals. The secret of developing excellence in whatever role we play in life is in consuming the right length of time in doing right things in the right way at the right time.

How Time is Spent

A professor was teaching the concept of time management to his students. A bag of sand, a bag of pebbles, some big rocks, a jug of water and bucket was used for demonstrating the concept by him.

> ***"the secret of getting the required time (or minutes) is not in finding time but in planning for it"***

> "*planning & prioritization are two vital components of time management*"

He asked the students, "What would you prefer to put into the bucket first?"

The students promptly said, "Water".

"Okay, what would you put next in the bucket?" asked the professor.

Most students said,"Sand".

"There lies a catch," said the professor. "These are easy things and need less effort. The tendency usually is to put these first. But you are forgetting a fact that by doing this your big rocks and pebbles will hardly have space left in the bucket. Similar to this, our day can be filled by trivial and low-value tasks, leaving important ones pending. Alternatively, we can plan and execute high-value tasks first, filling in the small unproductive intervals for trivial tasks.

He explained further, "If you put big rocks first, you always can put pebbles in the spaces and then sand can go in the remaining smaller spaces. Water can always be poured the last. This way you can maximise filling of the bucket."

The experiment beautifully teaches us the importance of planning and prioritisation. These are the two vital components of time management. Once you learn to master these, your performance and productivity will rise to new heights.

Just understand that what is interesting may not be useful and what is useful may not be interesting. Time management needs understanding the difference between the two and prioritising the useful more than interesting.

Let us begin with understanding the consumption of the concept called 'time'. Think about 'time' a bit and you will realise that you just measure movement and call it 'time'. Movement of the Earth around the Sun measures time as also by rotation on its own axis. We call these durations as one year and one day respectively.

In living these durations, the two factors that broadly influence our activities are 'urgency' and 'importance'. The activities that have an appearance of demanding our immediate attention are 'urgent'. The activities that advance us towards our goal, mission, or wish are 'important'.

Urgency syndrome is visible and acts on us for action; it has a low patience to wait. Ring of a telephone, doorbell, a note from the superior, an accident, or a crisis are examples of stimuli that we deal with urgently. Leaving aside the projects with deadlines, very often urgent matters do not advance us toward our plans. The urgency syndrome dominates actions, irrespective of the importance when goals are not clear and commitment is weak. Since important activities usually do not appear urgent, at least initially, these need a pro-active approach by taking an initiative to take the

> "*urgency syndrome dominates actions irrespective of the importance*"

> *Ineffective people engage in fire-fighting cousing waves & as a result create stress*

responsibility.

There is no precise point separating 'urgent' from 'not-urgent' or for that matter 'important' from 'not-important'. We can visualise a continuum having 'important' on one end and 'not important' on the other. For simplifying, let us make only two segments of both 'important' and 'urgent'.

Consumption of minutes and hours of any day can now be categorised into four combinations of importance and urgency. These are 'important-urgent'; 'important-not urgent'; 'not important-urgent' and 'not important-not urgent'. Let us discuss activities under each of the four combinations.

<u>Important-Urgent:</u> Activities usually are deadlines or crises. If it is a crisis, surely the attention was not given when the matter was not urgent. Many people develop an attitude of procrastination and waiting for an appropriate time. Our education and examination system promotes an attitude of doing things at the last moment. This attitude lingers on later in life and takes the shape of a similar approach in all walks of life. People with this attitude would unconsciously wait for the last moment and do things in urgency. If by chance such acts are appreciated, as usually happens so, this becomes a habit.

People doing important-urgent activities are very busy. Ineffective people engage in fire-fighting, causing waves and as a result create stress. Effective people plan and act well in advance for projects with deadlines. Our competency or management skills are at test when we deal with occasional crises beyond our control. However, excellence demands of us to keep our focus sharpened on activities that are important but not urgent to eliminate chances of creating crises due to procrastination or improper prioritisation.

For most people, planning, setting and achieving goals for their body, mind, soul, family, career and society are important activities that are not urgent and can wait. In waiting for an appropriate time later, they create crises. Remember, your success requires that you discourage an attitude of procrastination and waiting till the last moment for yourself and others around.

Important-Not Urgent: Activities need pro-active approach and initiative that comes through clarity of goals or mission. There are all reasons for calling this as a success combination. Successful people view life holistically and set goals in each dimension of life. This enables them to live a fulfilling and balanced life.

People engaged in important-not urgent activities are busy too but with a difference. They are busy in planning, executing the plans, relation building, re-creating and spending time on high-value tasks. These people are busy but enjoy peace of mind.

> *"people engaged in important-not urgent activities are busy but with peace of mind"*

Urgent–Not Important: activities are urgent but do not advance your goals or mission. Usually people doing

> *"not urgent & not important activities are a sure sign of failure"*

these activities are under the impression that they are into important things. What will others think, say or do dominates actions under our cultural conditioning. Remember, activities advancing the goal of someone else may not necessarily be important for you.

The other major reason people stay in this combination is that they lack the power of saying 'no'. Usually it is the absence of clarity in their mission or goals that makes people say 'yes' to not-important activities. They derive satisfaction of pleasing others at their own cost. They keep saying 'yes' to others and, in doing so, keep saying 'no' to themselves.

Not Urgent–Not Important: activities are a sure sign of failure. Many people give in to their habits and watch TV or listen to radio or read papers or engage in conversation or in games or chat on their mobile telephones without a clearly defined objective. Such people don't realise that once past, time will not come back.

Studies reveal that those who engage more in urgent and important fire-fighting tasks generally find an excuse in these activities as recreation. Question is how can anyone having wishes and dreams, mission and goal, spend even a minute on such activities? Obviously one major reason people engage in not-important and not-urgent activities is the unclear purpose of living life and absence of long or short-term goals. The other reason is absence of the commitment required to achieve their dreams.

Successful people, on the other hand, make conscious efforts to stay away from these. They know that to engage in activities that are neither urgent nor important is an act of insanity.

Time and Timing

Success comes to those who understand well that time is the key resource for achieving what they desire and deserve. Getting into the zone of excellence demands that you respect time and understand the dynamics of its management. We have limited time capital at our disposal, especially in relation to the vision and dreams we have for life. We will become more effective and productive if we spend our time on right things at the right time for the right length of time.

There are two aspects related to this key resource called 'time' to understand it a bit better. One describes it in the form of 'adequacy', the other as 'appropriateness'.

Work that is not executed at the right time for the right length of time can at best be called 'hard work'. Success demands doing 'smart work' - spending adequate time at appropriate time. Our daily activities need study and analysis before we decide what time is appropriate for which activities. These will have some relation to our goals, mission, or wishes. We need to prioritise our activities in order of the importance of the goals to decide how much of

> *"spend your time on right things at the right time for the right length of time."*

time we have to give for each of our goals.

Be aware that an exercise of finding appropriateness and adequacy is not an one-time activity. Choosing growth-over decline, we will challenge the status quo. We will enquire whether we are doing smart work on a regular basis, lest habits dictate our actions trapping us in hard work. Countless people spend time in reading newspapers, watching television, telephonic conversation, reading and writing e-mails and entertainment by habit more than the need.

Steps to Managing Time

<u>Finding worth of your time.</u> You must have heard: 'Time is money'. Is it true in application? It is not. You can see people wasting minutes liberally, but not rupees. Think of tearing off a currency note of even a rupee. Not easy. But think of wasting thirty minutes for gossiping. No problem.

Time and money are more of concepts than realities. We value these differently at different places. For example, rupees paid for helping a poor person appear higher than the same value spent in entertainment. Similarly time also is perceived differently at different occasions.

I say, "Time productively used is convertible into money", for time and money can be exchanged. Ask yourself what is the value of each minute of yours. It is very important to be conscious of time. Remember, money lost can be earned again, but once lost, time can never be.

People in employment find value of their each minute by dividing their present earning by the number of hours they work. Business people sometimes find the value by their contribution to the business divided by the number of hours they put in. You may also calculate the value of your each minute based on your potential, depending upon the competencies and opportunities around you. Yet another

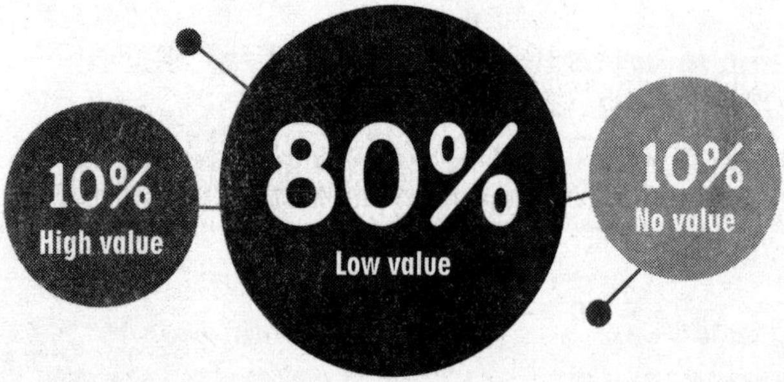

way to calculate the worth of your each minute is divide your desired income by the desired number of work-hours. Those who are not in employment, like housewives and students, can create their own measurements for valuing their minutes. The concept here is that be conscious of the worth of your each minute as you are of each rupee.

<u>Find out how you are spending your time at present</u>
It is important for you to know your current reality of time management. Use a log sheet on an hourly basis to note the activities your last hour was spent in. Now-a-days some cell phone apps are available that can help you track your time.

More than a century ago, economist Vilfredo Pareto enunciated a principle named after him as 'Pareto Principle' that specifies an unequal relationship between inputs and outputs. It is popularly known as 80:20.

By this, you may observe 20 per cent of invested input yields 80 per cent of the results obtained. Put another way, 80 per cent of consequences stem from 20 per cent of the causes. Applying this principle to time, you will notice that your 80 per cent time spent gives you 20 per cent results. tPut it the other way, your 20 per cent time gets you 80 per cent of the results. It will therefore be sensible to find the pattern of your time spent and eliminate those activities that contribute less to results.

I have enunciated my principle, namely Ten: Eighty: Ten (10:80:10). In relation to the time spent, you can notice that most people spend only 10 per cent of their time in activities that can be called high value. Eighty per cent of their time goes in doing low-value tasks. In fact most people are doing the work of their subordinates. Ten per cent of the time goes in activities that can be called no value or negative value activities.

High-value activities are those that carry higher value than the value of your time or ones that advance you towards your goals. Low-value activities have lower value than that of your minute or these activities are such that though these advance your goals, these can be done by others and not necessarily by you. No-value activities are those that have either no value or sometimes a negative value.

By logging your time, you will most likely conclude that 10 per cent of your time is spent in high value, 80 per cent in low value, and remaining 10 per cent in no value activities. If it is so, you are working hard, not smart. The key to success is in making efforts to increase your time in high-value activities by delegating some of the low value and deleting no-value activities.

You will, by logging your time, notice the pattern of its usage. Find out where your minutes are going. If you take care of your minutes, hours will be taken care of by themselves. In the growth phase, we keep changing our activities and, therefore, it is recommended that time logging must be done on a regular basis, say once every three months or so.

In relation to your career or profession or business, list all activities that you presently do. Classify these into three categories: High value, low value, no value.

Set long-tem and short-term goals in line with your 'mission' of life. Make long-term goals in line with your vision and mission of life that will move you to reality from your wish. It is useful and simpler initially, to make a mission statement for each area of life. The long-term goals can be say for ten or five years and must cover all areas of life in order to lead a fulfilling life. Break down the long-term goals to achieve them in one year, one month, one week as these periods approach. Your daily activities will then get automatically decided and aligned to your mission. Your goals will have their origin in your mission-for each area of your life.

> "*make a mission statement for each area of life*"

> "prioritizing your activities is an important part of your decision as to where to spend or invest time"

Your goals will also emanate from your wish list. Students and housewives can set annual goals in each area of their life. Students can further add goals in each subject depending upon their mission.

One way of finding goals in each area of your life is finding the unsatisfaction in that area. What more could be done and should be done to improve the existing situation or remove an existing pain in the area.

Prioritise your goals. Having made goals in each area of life based on your mission or wish or unsatisfaction, you may conclude that the available time of the day is not enough for achieving what you desire. In such a situation you will have to prioritise your goals, giving more priority to some over others, depending upon the situation you are in.

Life is a constant process of decision-making. Prioritising your activities is an important part of your decision as to where to spend or invest time. Prioritisation helps you move from doing 'first things first' to doing 'right thing at right time'. Making a choice to give priority to one goal over the other or one area over the other may be difficult at times. But, you are the best judge of deciding what needs to be taken first and what can wait for later. At such times your leadership quality of making a right decision will be at test. But prioritisation is important as it helps you decide the direction when it is time to determine where you want to go next.

Once you consciously prioritise your goals from all areas of your life, you will move toward doing smart work. You will be able to picture the desired results so clearly that you know how it will feel when these are achieved. You will then experience a sense of relief from stress arising out of doing hard work. In value terms, all those activities that move you towards your mission and goals in any area of your life are your high-value activities. All other activities are low value or no-value ones.

Our cultural values to sacrifice for others has conditioned us to 'give priority to others over self'. The return we get is some appreciation, at times, from others. Surely, such a message was not given with the intention that we sacrifice our goals for others. Such messages have actually not been interpreted right. Prioritisation must reflect that you are committed to your goals. Of course, while setting goals you keep in mind your responsibilities towards your institution, family and society. Giving priority to what you desire and deserve without the intention of hurting others you love is your right and privilege. Your duty to your goals demand you use your right to give priority to your goals over what others think, say, or do. When you give undue priority to others at the cost of your own goals, you stand to lose in your journey of success and fulfillment.

> "*giving priority to what your desire & deserve is your right & privilege*"

Make a timetable and add more high-value activities in your plan. For being effective in

> *while making your timetable, you must add more high value activities in each area of your life*

life and achieving excellence, it is important to engage in doing right things at appropriate time (when) for adequate time (how long). Making a timetable helps you plan your day, week, month and year in line with your goals that emerge out of your wish list or dissatisfaction in each area of life.

While making your timetable, you must add more high value activities in each area of your life. Remember high-value activities are those that advance your goals having value more than that of your time. Activities for developing your competencies in the direction of your long-term goals are very important high-value activities that need a very high degree of pro-active approach from your side.

When you incorporate more high-value activities into your day, you will need more time. Fact of life is that we all get limited one thousand four hundred forty minutes daily. You may conclude that a lot of low-value activities and no-value activities are filling your day. That is the time for you to take the sixth step.

Eliminate no value (NV) and delegate low value (LV) activities. Once you have added more of high-value activities in your plan, you will have pressure on your time. That is the moment you squeeze out the low value and no-value activities from your routine.

Remember habits die hard. Your rationalisation may fool you to justify what you are doing at present.

Challenge yourself, think of your unexplored potential and look at your goals in line with your wish list. Work continuously towards delegating the low-value activities. Eliminate your no-value activities. A word of caution here! Do not delegate your low-value activities or eliminate your no-value activities before adding high-value activities into your timetable. If you do so, you may reduce your work capacity by doing less in more time. Be careful about it.

Once you master your key resource called time, you will take control of your life. Excellence will then follow you.

❑

Motivation I Can I Will

Understanding Motivation

Motivation by Hope of Gain or Fear of Loss

Motivation I Can I Will

> "*motivation is a combination of two words: motiv(e) & a(c)tion*"

Understanding Motivation

I read a story some time ago that relates to the subject perfectly. A donkey was very disappointed the way his owner treated him and was frustrated with his life. Same work; same drudgery every day. There was nothing to wait for when the sun rose and morning came up. He spoke to his friend, another donkey, who looked very cheerful and enthusiastic and wanted to know the secret of his happiness.

The second donkey said, "I was also disappointed with my life like you are. In fact, I wanted to commit suicide. But an incidence of yesterday changed my thoughts and I am now convinced what life is.

"What happened yesterday?" asked the first donkey.

"You see, yesterday my owner was very angry. His only daughter, beautiful one, had done something wrong and there was a big argument going on. Finally before leaving his house, the owner said to his daughter, "If you don't mend your ways, I shall be forced to marry you to a donkey." From that moment onwards, I am expecting some miraculous restoring of luck on me and I am keeping myself fully prepared and motivated.

What is motivation? Read the word motivation as a combination of two words: motiv(e) and a(c)tion — Motive and Action! Yes, it is that simple. Motivation is nothing but action with a motive, a purpose. So, if you have a purpose, an objective, a goal together with action, you will be motivated. Hope makes the second donkey motivated.

Understand clearly that motivation is an internal process. You cannot motivate anyone else. You can inspire others. You can create conditions that can help people get motivated. Your journey of excellence can inspire many others and make them motivated, for they then have a motive to act.

If you are motivated, others may get inspired. When you help others act for their motives, they become motivated. Ask yourself, what motivates you; which situations, people, statements, actions motivate or de-motivate you. Your awareness of the factors that get you in such a state is very important for taking charge of the emotions you have at different times.

Motivation is the fuel for development and sustenance of excellence. You have to develop the eternal power and skill to motivate yourself on a continuous basis. When you take action for achievement of a goal, there are times when you are 'unsuccessful' and that may de-motivate you. Your vision and mission of your life, your wish list and your goals will provide the power of self-motivation at such a time. Many people think that successful people don't have setbacks. It is not true. The fact is that in spite of the setbacks they continue their journey based on their belief in themselves and the objective they have set.

> "*motivation is the fuel for development & sustenance of excellence*"

Let us understand a little more about motivation and needs of people that motivate them.

As understood until now, hierarchy of basic needs that seem to be universal motivators of human behaviour are:

Physical or biological,
Safety or security,
Social or love,
Ego or esteem, and
Self-actualisation or self-fulfilment.

Let us discuss these a bit more in detail.

Physical or Biological

It is considered as the lowest-level need that includes food, appearance and health. Physical needs are satisfied quickly. Very often, higher-level needs are attempted only when the physical needs are reasonably satisfied.

Safety or Security

Safety or security needs, such as shelter, work and assets are at the next level of needs. Many people feel quite insecure. Their security lies in building and in possession of assets.

You must understand that your real security is in you within your control. It is in your values, confidence, competencies and potential. Relationship, business, job and movable or immovable assets are only symbols of security. You may have all these things and still feel insecure. On the other side, you may lack these and still feel secure. It all depends on your perception. You have the power to see half-full and be secure and contented. You also have the power to see half-empty as unexplored potential in you.

By developing the skill of self-motivation 'I Can I Will' to explore more of your potential for a purpose, you will develop excellence in whatever you do with a sense of security.

Social or Love

The next level of human needs is the thirst for social acceptance and love. These needs are temporarily fulfilled through having all that which symbolises them.

You must understand here that usually the need for social acceptance is rooted in a deeper need of self-acceptance. As you work through achieving excellence, you will experience that your self-acceptance will grow by using more of your unexplored potential for the purpose in your mind. Comparing your achievements, position and possessions with those of others will become irrelevant (or very little relevant) then.

Ego or Esteem

The next higher-level need is of ego and self–esteem that demand you to prove your worthiness mostly through public notice and recognition.

> "*the need for social acceptance is rooted in a deeper need of self-acceptance*"

the need for social acceptance is rooted in a deeper need of self-acceptance

When you will have improved clarity of purpose of

> *life is a process of evolution, self-actualization & value addition.*

your living, present position and vast unexplored potential and when you learn to motivate yourself through 'I Can I Will', your ego needs will then get satisfied in doing your best and in doing what challenges you by using more of your potential for the purpose.

Self-actualisation or Self-fulfilment

Self-actualisation or self-fulfilment needs are a movement toward being a 'fulfilled person'. In this state, things happen and sometimes you may realize that you are not a doer. Life is a process of evolution, self-actualisation and value addition. Understanding this helps you attain higher levels of mental and spiritual development that strengthen your commitment to be excellent in whatever you choose to do. Many people believe that the self–fulfilment need gets attention only after all other lower-level needs are moderately satisfied. Study of lives of great leaders defies this belief. Clarity of mission of your life can surely lead you to this level even though your physical safety, social acceptance and ego needs have not been completely satisfied.

Understanding the hierarchy of needs is important. It makes you aware of the level you think you stand as of now. In addition, you come to realise the gap between the present state and the state you intend to reach. Understanding the hierarchy also provides an understanding of general human behaviour that will be useful when you inspire people around you.

Let us now look at some of the ways you can use motivation to develop your leadership. You may very well be aware that the prime drivers of human endeavour are 'hope of gain' or 'fear of loss'. We experience these motivators from an early age. The underlying principle governing these motivators is trade-off. Trade-off implies that nothing is free. You get something by paying the price for it. There is always a trade-off between the expectation and the payable price. The expectation includes the benefit to be achieved or loss to be avoided while the payable price may be in terms of money or effort or time. Both these motivators are, however, not powerful for self–motivation and development of leadership. Moreover, these motivators are external and temporary in nature. Let us discuss both these motivators in a little more detail.

Motivation by 'Fear of Loss'

This type of motivation is popularly known as 'X' (Douglas McGregor theory) or 'stick' and is one of the oldest type of motivations that drives us to act for fear of some negative or undesirable consequences.

Almost all religions use this type of motivation. Societal norms are implemented with a fear in mind that violation will meet with adverse consequences. Families use fear with children for maintaining discipline and customs set by elders.

> *"both 'hope of gain' & 'fear of loss' are not powerful motivations for self-motivation & development of leadership"*

> "*fear motivation is negative & damaging in nature, though it does give immediate result*"

Though fear motivation is negative and damaging in nature, it does give immediate results. Comparatively speaking, the fear of loss is more powerful and instantaneous than the hope of gain. But, fear holds back creativity and slows down efforts. In an environment of fear, people become unsure of their actions. They become dependent and inefficient. Their approach to a task becomes defensive and they develop insensitivity to the needs of others. They evade the responsibility of decision making. They lose confidence and develop tolerance to the punishment and find ways out in psychological defences. Thus, any benefits of fear motivation are temporary, especially if fear is used indiscriminately or injudiciously.

Motivation by 'Hope of Gain'

Popularly known as 'Y' (Douglas McGregor theory) or 'carrot' or 'incentive', this type of motivation promises tangible or intangible rewards as a trade-off for compliance. It is used in families, societies and religious institutions to the extent that the benefits of an action in the present can accrue in the next life. Carrot motivation works best when the carrot is juicy and the person is hungry.

The incentive motivation is a function of the need and greed of the person to be motivated. If these are missing or weak, this type of motivation is ineffective. Moreover, with the passage of time, it becomes less attractive; sometimes people get used to the rewards and develop a tendency to view the reward as their right or entitlement.

Though there is nothing inherently wrong with wanting to be rewarded, this type of motivation does not satisfy your need to explore your potential to be excellent in whatever you do and develop your leadership. Incentive motivation does not inspire you to be as great as you can be.

You work hard to achieve monetary gain or recognition or growth. And you may, at the same time, be conscious that if you do not perform as required, you could lose reputation, financial security and self-respect. You can observe that both — hope of gain and fear of loss — are operative in some proportion.

In actual fact, most people are generally driven by a combination of these two types of motivation (X and Y), popularly known as 'Z' (William Ouchis theory).

Motivation- 'I Can I Will'

'Fear motivation' or 'incentive motivation' or a combination of the two has limited applications. These types of motivations are effective for a short duration for some situations. Being external in nature, their effectiveness will depend upon your overall objective for using them.

> *"incentive motivation does not inspire you to be as great as you can be"*

Developing excellence and leadership demands that you do not get unduly influenced by any combination of fear and hope.

Some mechanism to charge up self is required for being in control. It demands you to focus on the potential you have and the possibilities you can create. It is internal and is not unduly influenced by external factors. Thus, excellence demands motivating yourself through another type of motivation captured in 'I can' (potential) and 'I will' (commitment).

'I can' suggests that there are possibilities and potential. It is based on the understanding that if there is a wish in mind, there is a matching potential too that can be harnessed to make the wish a reality. Regular affirmation of "I Can" will make you think and gradually believe that you are endowed with powers matching your dreams and desires.

'I will' suggests that there is a need to bring in a commitment for making your wish a reality. The commitment flows out of building competencies and developing a will to do. Regular affirmation of "I Will" makes you comfortable in entering and sustaining in your "Uncomfort Zone".

Development of excellence is an exercise in 'I Can I Will' motivation that begins with your realisation that you have vast potential that can be explored and you are committed to achieving your dreams. Regular affirmation of 'I Can I Will' makes you shift your perception from scarcity to abundance. It makes you create your life the way you desire rather than the way others want it to be. Such perception helps you develop an attitude of commitment to surpass your own achievements continuously. This attitude comes by your realisation that human potential is unlimited and the world is abundant with opportunities. Once you appreciate these, it makes you commit to your dreams with full confidence. You also realise that you have what it takes to make your dream turn into reality. You then become focussed on what you think is right for you and become invulnerable to what others think, say or do. You also start questioning the self-imposed limitations that you have accepted by wayof conditioning by others or your own experiences.

Here, it is important for you to realise that you have acquired your perception, attitude and habits over the years. Though you had very little control over the environment that supported creation of these perceptions, attitudes and habits, now you can make a choice to change. Of course, dealing with deep-seated perceptions, attitudes and habits formed over a number of years, is sure to take some time. You need extra power of persistence as captured in the following lines:

Events will not unfold your way, mostly or a bit;
Leadership is finding alternatives and ways to persist.
Think 'I Can I Will'.

Path of your success neither is certain nor amply lit;
Leadership is taking risk and having courage to persist.
Think 'I Can I Will'.

> *Once the I Can-I Will motivations is in you, you will find no challenge big enough to stop you from moving toward your dreams*

Your heart will say 'go-on' and mind commands to 'quit';
Leadership is following your heart and conviction to persist.

Think 'I Can I Will'.

People around will not always acknowledge your grit
Leadership is exploring potential and belief to persist.

Think 'I Can I Will'.

'I Can I Will' motivation also follows the trade-off principle. However, there is a little difference in sequencing the action and end results. The commitment to review your perception, examine your attitudes and challenge your habits will have to take place NOW. The hope of gain or fear of loss will fructify later. The results are time consuming but need a price to be paid beforehand. That is one reason that the motivation 'I Can I Will' grows on you slowly. You have to believe that you are not trading-off something for nothing. You follow the law of nature: Sow now, reap later.

Once the I Can I Will motivation is in you, you will find no challenge big enough to stop you from moving towards your dreams. Excellence will become part of your living then. Your leadership position will get strengthened then.

Just remember: You Can, if You Will

❑❑❑